MW01483855

Challenge of The Keys

Challenge of The Keys

by Jane Leazer

Knoxville, Tennessee, USA
crippledbeaglepublishing.com

Cover art by Jolene Scheepers
Cover design by Maria Loysa-Bel Nueve-de los Angeles
Edited by Kourtney Schmiedeke and Jody Dyer

Paperback ISBN 978-1-958533-67-3
Hardcover ISBN 978-1-958533-66-6

Library of Congress Control Number: 2024900872

Printed in the United States of America

Challenge of The Keys is dedicated with much love and deep appreciation to my granddaughter, Gracie Hamlett. Gracie played an instrumental role in shaping the storyline and setting, breathing life into the main characters. I am profoundly grateful for her remarkable creativity, vivid imagination, and keen editing skills, as well as her unwavering enthusiasm and encouraging support.

With love,
Mimi

PROLOGUE

In the quiet depths of history, five exceptional bloodlines concealed a cryptic link to a shadowy institution known as the enigmatic Academy.

Allie, a young woman possessed of the incredible power of telekinesis, had always been drawn to the unspoken legacy woven into her family's past.

Kit, a rare talent in the art of teleportation, felt an insatiable urge to explore realms far beyond her tranquil town.

Christan, with his uncanny knack for deciphering body language and emotions, often pondered why he could sense what others couldn't.

Then there were Aiden and Amaya, twins wielding metaphysical powers over water and fire, their elemental abilities shrouded in awe and mystery.

Little did they know, their extraordinary gifts were not mere happenstance but threads intricately woven into a concealed realm—a world steeped in magic and enigma.

As they approached the age when family secrets were destined to be unveiled, cryptic letters arrived, each addressed to a single recipient.

These letters would change their lives forever, setting them on a path to the Academy, an institution that held the key to unlocking their potential and understanding their heritage.

Within the Academy's hallowed halls lay not only the secrets of their lineage but also challenges that would test their character, knowledge, imagination, loyalty, and their ability to support one another.

Their journey would not only be about mastering their extraordinary abilities but also discovering the depths of their own hearts. The truth, they would soon realize, was not found in right or wrong answers but in the very essence of their being.

As the letters beckoned them towards an unimaginable destiny, the door to adventure creaked open, revealing a world brimming with wonder, peril, and the promise of self-discovery.

Their path remained uncertain, but their bond was unbreakable. b Together, they would confront the trials awaiting them at the Academy and beyond.

Each would look within their heart and mind, thereby truth they would find. Although they didn't know what would happen next, their strong friendship would empower them to overcome the challenges they'd encounter at the Academy.

WHENCE IT ALL BEGAN: FAMILY

A THUNDEROUS BOOM SHOOK MY ROOF AND STARTLED ME AWAKE. The sky was still dark, but dawn was approaching. With my 360-degree panoramic view, I considered standing on my balcony to observe the storm rolling in. However, I wisely chose not to tempt fate, especially with my birthday just around the corner. After all, it would be here soon.

On the east side of my view, droplets pelted my windows. Soon, a wall of water rained down, creating puddles on my balcony. As the storm raged, I detected scents of cinnamon and the aroma of coffee wafting up through the grate in my floor, tempting me to rise and head downstairs.

Due to the downpour, I could barely hear my Mum and Mimi chatting, but I did manage to catch some mention of my upcoming birthday. By now, I was eager to learn more about the plans for my twelfth birthday, and I hoped to discover them over breakfast.

As I rose and made my bed, I thought about how my room was once my Mum's, Grandmother Mimi's and Great Grand Rie's bedroom. Mimi, my Mum and I were born in our grand home having been delivered by a midwife. morning, I felt the presence of my Great grandmother Rie and the sweet matriarchs who shared this space

Hanging on a clothes tree in the corner was a silk woven shawl created by my Grand Rie back in the 1950's, with a feathered cloche from the same time period perched on top. Photos of me as a little girl dressing up in her attire adorned the walls. These, along with many family photos, dotted the surrounding walls. Paintings and pottery created by Mum and Mimi were strategically placed around my expansive room. These treasures surrounded and comforted me.

The grate, open as always, served as a valuable source of information. When older homes were built, contractors installed grates to allow warm air to travel from room to room, but I found them more useful for eavesdropping on conversations and picking up information. I remembered one time when I overheard one of my teachers discussing me with Mum about me being a child prodigy. I was three at the time, so I asked her what that meant, and she explained that a prodigy is someone curious, smart, creative, and ahead of his or her age. Her response satisfied my curiosity. Knowing that I was a child prodigy didn't surprise Mum and Mimi. I didn't attend a traditional school but participated in homeschool and accelerated programs. Other children were involved as well since my parents recognized the importance of social development.

Traveling was a significant part of my education, and my portfolio was expansive. My Mum owned a flat in the city where she also had a gallery. Mum, Mimi, and I took frequent excursions into the city to enjoy events showing their art, attend the theater, or dine at the opening of posh restaurants.

Traveling by train was my favorite mode of transportation. Sometimes, we even stayed overnight in sleeper cars, and the dining cars were amazing. Traveling out West on Amtrak, we experienced a magnificent view of the open skyline. As the train clipped along, we heard the porter call out the name of each town just before the train arrived. It was a great adventure, and our most enjoyable moments occurred when we hopped between cars to make our way to the dining car for breakfast. We all marveled at the refined cuisine offered to us as we journeyed into the rugged West. My second favorite mode of travel was sailing on an ocean liner. Watching the sunrise and sunsets awakened my senses and tested my artistic and photographic skills.

My great-grand and great-grandpapa met on a liner as they crossed the "pond" to migrate to the United States of America. Marie DuBois, my Great-Grand, designed hats while Edward Briggsman, my Great Grandpapa, was a photographer and inventor. Grand grew up in Paris, France, while Grandpapa resided in London, England. Both were youngsters when World War II broke out and ravaged their cities. Once the war commenced, their parents sent them to their country estates for safety.

Grandpapa recounted times when, late at night, he listened to Chancellor Winston Churchill's encouraging and patriotic speeches on the radio. All the citizens clung to Churchill's comforting words during the time of great peril. My Grand shared that the French resistance often stayed at their estate and told her riveting stories about encounters with the enemy. Grand and Grandpapa remembered their excitement and their feelings of exhilaration when France and England were liberated. Their stories enthralled me, as did their photos documenting their freedom. As their careers blossomed, each decided to migrate to America.

They loved the ocean and believed that traveling by liner across the pond was a wise move for a young adult in pursuit of their dreams. *That is how they met!* Both my Grandpapa and Grand were affluent, and family documents suggested that they may have had aristocratic ties. Lord Briggsman was my Grandpapa Edward's father, and he lived on an estate outside of London. Grand's family were distant cousins of nobility dating back to the 1800s. Rie, as Grand was called, lived in a suite in Paris and spent her summers in the countryside. Clearly, her roots in fashion were inspired by her historic lineage. Both were young and talented. On board, they were seated at the same dining table and placed next to each other. Fate played its hand, and love blossomed in the salty air.

Grandpapa snapped countless photos that filled many albums. Two generations later, as was their great-granddaughter, I loved browsing through the pages with Mum and Mimi. Later, as I read Grand's exposé about their courtship, I chuckled at her ploys to just happen to be wherever Grandpapa appeared. All of the women bellylaughed at Grand's description of how she swooned each time she encountered Grandpapa. She frequently commented on his charm and good looks. The series of photos was a visual account of sparks igniting into a growing, passionate love.

By the time they arrived in New York City, Grandpapa had proposed, and their engagement was short-lived as they had eloped. Often Mum, Mimi, and I poured through their albums and journals filled with fraying pages while we imagined their story as a poetic romantic novel. Though they both loved city life, they wanted to start a family. My Grandpapa and Grand had spent most of their childhood by the sea and sought to locate a home along the coast. They hoped to find a coastal home outside a city where they could build their careers and raise a family.

Fortunately, they found a magnificent home of great character off the coastal highway near Charleston, South Carolina. It was perched on a slight bluff with a glorious view of the ocean and was listed on the historic registry. The three-story house had a turret perched on the top floor, which was converted into a bedroom. The original wood floors were refurbished, and tiles from Italy and France adorned the bathrooms and adorned the kitchen walls. Worn shutters were replaced, and the walls were painted with bright colors reflecting their moods. Shades covering the windows filtered out the light on bright and sunny days.

Grand's studio was later transformed into a sunroom where all the females in the house created works of art. Grandpapa enjoyed growing plants, so a hot house emerged, housing exotic flowers and strawberries that still grow to this day.

My favorite room is the den, which we converted into our library. On one shelf, there are rows of colorful glass French perfume bottles that paint the walls with rainbows on a sunny day. Many trinkets from travels abroad, quilts, silk afghans, capes, and paraphernalia, created by family artists, filled every space and draped over plush chairs. Of course, there were shelves of books, including classics, and some first editions. Grand's French provincial desk, an heirloom, was the focal point. An antique and priceless, its value was more about the legacy. As a little tyke, I pried open a few drawers; however, some spaces remained locked and unavailable to me. Being ever so curious, I'd asked Mum and Mimi why it was locked, but all they did was smile, explaining that one day they would open them up and allow me to discover the treasures held within.

The historical component of our home added to the charm and warmth of each room. The character of the home reflects those who reside there. My home was influenced by the strength of the Briggsman female household. Both my Grandpapa and Grand, whom I called Rie when I was small, lived long lives and helped raise me along with Mum and Mimi. I can still hear their laughter and fondly remember story time at bedtime, painting, and finding shells on the beach after a storm. "The best time to find them," Grandpapa would say. Later, he would browse through an old, tattered book about shells and find the exact name of the unique shell we had found. We'd walk, talk, and take photos, as he took extra time explaining how to filter the light, teaching me so much.

So many favorite photos are framed and hung on my bedroom walls, as well as being displayed in many an album. Rie was an accomplished designer, and fragments of fabrics could be found in many a basket. I created many clothes for my dolls and for myself as well! Most were quite attractive, colorful, and fun!

Naturally, being French, Rie was an accomplished cook and baker. Mum and Mimi were equally well-versed in cooking and, best of all, baking. Early on, I learned that baking is scientific and precise. Rie taught me how to measure and knead the dough to the exact point of perfection. Grandpapa would enter the kitchen just as we removed a brioche from the oven. Yes, I could make an amazing cheese soufflé that was just as delicious as Rie's.

Though we loved nesting in our grand beach home, we all traveled together to France, eating our way around cafes, patisseries, and into the countryside, where we visited estates and farms. London was so much fun, and I enjoyed being a tourist, visiting the castle and museums, as well as partaking in high tea at the palace. Grandpapa's dignitaries and Lords shared tea with us and gave us a tour of the palace. Over our many years together, we shared so many wonderful memories. They both passed away within a week of each other, peacefully in their sleep. Everywhere I look, I see and feel their presence. I miss them so much every day.

Now we remain a household of amazing and strong women. I don't remember my father, who passed away shortly after my birth. Taylor Jenkins, Mimi's husband, had passed away prior to my being born. Photos reveal that the two men were handsome, talented, loving, and wonderful whose legacies are written down in journals. Both my Granddad and father were well-known adventurers.

Mimi's husband met her when she was traveling abroad. The women in our family seem to fall hard and quickly in love. They fell in love and were married on the coast at our beloved home. Since the house had plenty of room, Mimi and Taylor moved in, and when Mum was born, the household was filled with happiness.

Sadly, Taylor died soon thereafter, and Rie and Grandpapa helped raise Mum. My father, Tony Reddinger, met Mum at college. He too was a photographer and was auditing a class where, by chance, he met his future wife, my Mum. Mum shares with a blush that she fell head over heels in love, and he did as well. Since my father owned his plane, they eloped and also returned to the homestead by the beach. Tragically, he passed away while on a flight. Just like the other amazing women and their documented photos, Tony and Mum were a beautiful couple, so in love. Sadly, he died before I was born. I resemble my father somewhat, but I am a "spittin" image of Rie.

Upstairs, I heard Mum and Mimi chatting. Most of the time, information funneled up through the grate was clear, yet their tones were hushed. I did detect some comments about my upcoming

16

birthday. *Travel plans?* Sweet scents beckoned me. I needed to check in with them.

As I entered the kitchen, the sun was filtering through the shades, and the French doors were open, leading out onto our wraparound porch. Double rainbows were forming in the sky over the horizon. *I have been told that the sight of a double rainbow could be a promising sign, perhaps connecting to my upcoming birthday.*

Mimi and Mum had prepared quite a spread for breakfast. So many choices were laid out, including my favorite brioche, baguette, creamy butter, brie, crème fraiche, honey from local hives, homemade preserves, and French-pressed coffee. *Could this delectable breakfast be an early celebration for me?*

I wondered and asked, "Mum, Mimi, what are my birthday plans?"

Both smiled exclaimed in unison, "Later!" Each looked like the Cheshire Cat that had swallowed the canary.

Back in my room, I checked out my telescope and noticed that the postman's truck was winding around the highway, apparently heading up our driveway. Hearing the doorbell, I hastily ran down the creaking steps from my bedroom.

I opened the door just in time for the postman to hand me a weathered, thick envelope.

"For you, but the return address is hard to read," he said.

I thanked him and yelled to Mum and Mimi, who took the envelope stating," You can open it later in Rie's library."

We had eaten supper, and as dusk approached, I entered Rie's library. There was a warm glow from multiple lit candles, instilling an air of mystery.

"Before you open the envelope, Allie, Mimi, and I will unlock a special drawer in Rie's desk," said Mum.

Whoa, I thought as I watched Mimi push a compartment that sprang open, and she took a key off a chain around her neck.

"Here, Allie is your first key to assist you with a challenge."

Challenge? Okay, I thought, while turning the key as the drawer opened. Inside was a letter addressed to me, as well as several letters and journals.

RIE'S LETTER

Dearest Allie,

Grandpapa and I wish we were there to celebrate your twelfth birthday. Our time with you was ever so special. Shortly before your birthday, you will receive an envelope. When you open it, you will start an amazing journey. At the age of twelve, I experienced a similar journey while growing up in France. Like you, my parents were told that I was a child prodigy. I was sent to a special Academy to develop my artistry and clairvoyant abilities. You can use my letters and journals at a later point to provide some guidance as you embark on your journey. Here is a gift to celebrate your twelfth birthday. An amazing journey awaits you.

Much love,
Rie

Mum handed me the tissue-wrapped gold box with a shiny ribboned bow. I felt breathless as I opened the box and saw a gold heart-shaped locket on a chain.

Inscribed was a message from Rie, "Allie, look deep inside your heart and mind, and there, truth you will find." Cursive letters *MB* were inscribed on the back. Tissues were passed around as we sniffled and hugged one another. There were no dry eyes in the room. I strongly felt Rie's presence as we placed the locket around my neck, and Mum clasped it. With all the excitement and emotion, Mum suggested that tomorrow would be a better time to open up my bulky envelope and start my journey as Rie indicated.

MY JOURNEY BEGINS: THE KEYS

I'M NOT SURE WHAT WOKE ME. My covers were tumbled about, and some had fallen on the floor. Filtered light danced across my walls, and I could hear the waves crashing on the coast. Perhaps a storm was brewing, and the outside noise paralleled the excitement mounting within me.

Maybe I was hungry, as sweet aromas sifted up through the grate from our kitchen. Mimi had baked a brioche, honoring a favorite recipe of Rie's. After all, she was front and center based on the preceding events unveiled.

A warm feeling came over me as I thought about her sweet letter to me. I clutched the heart locket, opened it, and read the inscription, "Look deep in your heart and mind; there truth you will find."

Today would be an incredible day! I hurried downstairs and entered the kitchen, where Mum and Mimi greeted me.

"Hungry?" Mum asked.

"Starving!" I exclaimed.

Mum declared, "I thought you might need a feast today; some food for your brain." She smiled broadly.

There was quite a spread, including my favorite spinach quiche, brioche, chocolate croissants, hot-house strawberries, and a coffee latte. "*Yum!*"

Being full and satisfied, I felt that I possessed the energy to approach and tackle my awaited task. Not knowing what to expect, I couldn't wait to get started.

Excited, we were ready to return to our library where Rie's journal was still placed on her vintage desk brought over from France so many years ago. Also to be opened was the bulky, weathered envelope addressed to me, which had arrived the day before. The envelope looked old, and no one could decipher the return address.

I remembered what Rie had written me, informing me that I would receive such an envelope. She was correct, and there it was right before my eyes.

Rie had shared that she possessed telepathic skills. Perhaps I had them too. When I was little, I remember experiencing head noise. Rie taught me to breathe and focus. Sometimes she put headphones on me, and we would paint. I needed to check into Rie's skills and perhaps discover my own abilities. Now it was time to open my envelope.

Opening the envelope, my stomach churned a little bit, feeling somewhat anxious, but more excited with anticipation. Inside, I found two letters written to me. One provided some cursory instructions, and the second letter explained why I received the letter and the challenges.

THE INVITATION

March 6, 2022

Dear Ms. Allie Reddinger,

Allie, BETA is pleased to recognize you as a possible candidate to attend our prestigious Academy. The proposed challenge is outlined in your invitation. You are permitted to remain at home to complete each challenge.

Since you are quite adept with your computer abilities, your answers can be sent using that format. The Academy is aware of your amazing ancestry and legacy relating to your Great Grandmother, Marie Dubois's telepathic skills and clairvoyance. You may have acquired similar abilities, but that is yet to be seen.

Keep in mind her advice as you make your decision; "Look in your heart and mind, and truth you will find."

Sincerely and Best Wishes,
Council of BETA

MUM AND MIMI REMAINED SILENT. I smiled at them and said, "I will sit on the porch and consider my possibilities and determine if I possess the abilities and confidence to proceed."

I smiled again as I shrugged my shoulders. I headed out and sat on the porch, rocking in a plush wicker chair.

Soon I sensed Rie's presence, yet I knew now this was about me. I opened the envelope and took out the next letter and started to read.

THE LETTERS

March 6, 2022

Dear Ms. Reddinger,

Allie, as stated in our invitation, it has come to our attention that you may be a potential candidate to attend BETA. Our Council has received recommendations from noteworthy individuals from your community and other notable authorities. To be selected as a BETA, you must master The 4 Keys. Each challenge will require you to answer a series of questions. If you are successful and answer each key to the Academy, you will be accepted to enter and to attend.

The 4 Key Challenges are:
- *Key of Character*
- *Key of Knowledge*
- *Key of Imagination*
- *Key of Loyalty*

27

If you accept this challenge, remember:

"Our questions will never trick. Answers you will be able to pick. Think deep in your heart and mind, and correct answers you will find!"

Sincerely and Best Wishes,
Council for BETA

I called out to Mum and Mimi. "I read the challenge and plan to accept!"

On my laptop, I accepted and pressed send. We all grinned, wondering what next to expect.

The next morning, I woke up all snuggled under my covers. Sunlight filled my room, waking me from a deep sleep. Aromas of coffee and cinnamon beckoned me as my tummy grumbled. A new day was upon me, and there was no telling what might happen.

As I started down the stairs, the doorbell rang. I almost stumbled as I hastened to the door. Looking through the beveled glass, I saw our postman.

"Allie, here's another envelope for you. Still not sure of the postmark." he said

"Thanks," I said to him, taking it and clutching the envelope.

"Mum, Mimi, another envelope arrived!"

I sat down on a rocker, opened it, and took a deep breath…

March 7, 2022

Ms. Reddinger,

Allie, BETA is delighted that you have accepted the Challenge of The 4 Keys. The first one is the Key of Character.

Our learned members are aware that you have researched scholars and learned about their character. As you have read, Merlin was a great clairvoyant who mentored King Arthur many centuries ago in England. Merlin's character was beyond reproach, and there are multiple character traits that describe him, including being selfless, protective, honorable, trustworthy, kind, caring, compassionate, brave, courageous, intelligent, perceptive and wise. Each trait is formidable, yet we have selected four prominent ones:

Courage: Doing the right thing.
Perception: Seeing the big picture.
Trustworthiness: Developing a strong bond.
Compassion: Caring for others.

Allie, your challenge to earn your first key is to determine which character trait is most important.

Remember, this question is not a trick. The correct answer is yours to pick. Dig deep in your heart and mind; surely the correct answer you will find!

We have great confidence in you.

Sincerely and Best Wishes,
Council for BETA

As I sat contemplating the impending challenge awaiting me, I took out a notebook and began jotting down some thoughts. Fiddling with my locket, I focused on Rie, who had experienced a similar journey decades before. My notes were outlined as follows:

She was twelve, living in France, and was privileged. During World War II, her family sent her to the countryside for protection. The French Resistance hid on their property, and Rie displayed bravery and helping their cause.

Grandpapa lived in London, and his father was a Lord. He too was privileged. During the Great War, he listened to Chancellor Churchill and documented the war through photography. At times, he was sent to their country estate to ensure his safety.

Later, after starting their careers, Rie and Grandpapa sailed on a liner to New York. While sailing, Rie and Grandpapa fell in love and married. They eventually moved South to our beach home.

Mimi was born. She grew up to become an artist and married a photographer who sadly passed away at a young age.

My Mum was born in our beach home. She too was an artist and married young. My father was a man of adventure, an explorer, and a pilot. I was born, but my father, like my granddad, died early in a plane crash. Grandpapa and Rie played a significant role in helping to raise me. I bore a striking resemblance to Rie and inherited her artistic talents. Sadly, they both passed away when I was young, and I now live in a household of strong women.

Now, I needed to summarize my thoughts into an essay that would answer the question of which trait is the most important in relation to the first Key of Character.

Reviewing my notes, I decided to take my time to respond to each trait and determine the correct response. The Council stated that there is no trick; the correct answer I can pick.

Rie's guidance echoed in my mind, urging me to look within my heart and mind, and there, the truth I will find. Encouraged, I took out my laptop and logged into my account to compose my answer.

March 7, 2022

Dear Council for BETA,

I have been told by my Mum, Grandmother Mimi, Great Grandmother Rie, my Grandpapa, teachers, and other significant people in my life that character matters. You have asked which trait is most important.

I will first address courage. My Great Grandparents lived during World War II and helped those in need under extreme circumstances and at great risk. Later, they crossed the ocean and began their careers within a competitive market, where they succeeded.

After moving South, my Mimi was born, and she became an artist. My Mum was born into a loving family, yet they both faced losses and displayed great courage as their careers flourished while raising me. All of the strong women in my life experienced hardships but consistently did the right thing, approaching each challenge with courage.

Secondly, perception is a trait of great importance. My family has always assessed various aspects when making decisions. We analyze, synthesize, and formulate facts while seeing the big picture.

Being trustworthy is an inherent trait in my family's heritage, founded on the development of strong bonds. Rie possessed telepathic abilities that she undoubtedly used to develop strong bonds with others. Both she and my Grandpapa were trusted by many, especially when they and their families assisted countrymen during World War II, establishing strong bonds. When they journeyed across the pond to the United States, they formed strong connections, marrying and building their lives together. When making decisions, they trusted each other to decide the best approach and move forward. I learned early in my life to trust others and create strong bonds based on that trust.

Being compassionate and caring for others was instilled in me from a young age. My family's legacy is based on helping others. Our family has established foundations, and Mum and Mimi have encouraged me to perform random acts of kindness. I always find simple ways to give back, like cleaning up the beach, tutoring, participating in bake sales, and helping food banks. We all have lots to share.

After considering these traits pertaining to one's character and providing supportive analysis, my conclusion is that being courageous, perceptive, trustworthy and compassionate are equally important.

No single trait is more important than the others. That is the truth upon which I base my answer.

I appreciate your confidence in me.

Sincerely,
Allie Reddinger

I pushed send. Now I had to wait. *Would they send a letter back online, or would I receive a letter?* Tired, I started hearing some head noise and chose to put on my headphones, covered myself with an afghan knitted by Rie, and fell asleep in a wicker rocking chair.

I felt Mum's gentle touch as she woke me up. Wonderful aromas wafted my way from our kitchen.

"Hungry?" Mum asked.

Nodding, I headed to the table laden with yummy bread, cheese, and a tureen of chicken noodle soup. Neither Mum nor Mimi prodded me about my response, anticipating that I would share a little bit with them.

Fiddling with Rie's locket, I smiled and said, "I really thought about the topic and the influence both of you and Rie had in my life. I know that my essay specifies an honest response, as I remembered Rie's words about seeking truth deep in my heart and mind. Now I have to wait and see if I can continue." I sounded somewhat confident, I thought.

Mum and Mimi smiled and both gave me big hugs and kisses. Soon, I chose to read in my room after taking a long, hot, relaxing bubble bath. The gentle chimes on my balcony lulled me to sleep.

Morning sun danced across my covers, providing a soft rainbow on my walls. I could barely hear the ocean and wondered if I should head out for a walk on the beach. I threw on my sweats and ball cap. Prior to starting down the stairs, the doorbell rang.

Shouting, "I'll get it!" I was greeted by the postman.

"Here you go, Allie." Once again, he handed me a weathered envelope without a clear postage. I thanked him, and off he went.

Mum and Mimi were already in the kitchen.

Entering, I questioned, "Perhaps the Academy has already responded?"

They both knew that I was anxious. On a tray, I placed some juice and a buttery brioche and headed for the porch.

I opened the envelope and read.

March 8, 2022

Dear Ms. Reddinger,

33

Allie, we have received your first response to the Challenge of The Keys. The Council plans to share your success once you respond to each key challenge. We are pleased by your deep thought process and honest answers and encourage you to follow the same methodology as you move forward.

Your next key challenge is the Key of Knowledge. The Council recognizes your stellar skills, excellent grades, honors, and awards received.

The Keys of Knowledge are as follows:
Quest: Desire to learn
Perseverance: Steadfast in spite of difficulty
Application: Implement and utilize

Allie, the challenge to access your second key, like the first, is knowing there are no tricks, and the correct answer you can pick. Continue to look in your heart and mind, knowing the correct answer you will find.

The Council applauds your forthright approach.

Sincerely and Best Wishes,
Council for BETA

Since it was pleasant in the sunroom, I took my laptop and opened it to my folder addressing challenges. My thoughts flowed.

My recollection of my desire to learn stems from vivid memories of my childhood and stories shared. I recall being described as a child prodigy and asking what that meant. Yes, I was curious, and my spoken language surpassed my chronological age. Reading was easy for me, and I could do so before I was four.

Clearly, I was one of those inquisitive children asking "Who, What, When, and Why?" Through our explorations and travels, I gleaned much knowledge as well by my creative, artistic, and culinary efforts. Perhaps high on my list would be that I am an avid reader.

Surely, being steadfast even when faced with difficulties brings to mind my many family losses, especially at a young age. Though being considered bright and somewhat exceptional, learning to be accepted by others and forming friendships required commitment.

Most certainly, I recall that learning and application would result in one's ability to implement and utilize these skills.

Before I drafted my response, I went to the kitchen and found the sandwich Mum had placed in the fridge. A bowl of strawberries sat on the counter by a jar filled with peanut butter cookies. Sitting on a stool, I chowed down.

Now it was time to resume my challenge.

I opened the page to respond.

March 8, 2022

Dear Council for BETA,

When I was a little girl, I uncovered that I was a child prodigy. My Mum explained that meant I was smart and could learn easily. Though I could acquire facts quickly, my family wanted to foster my desire to learn.

We were a family of means, and ample opportunities were afforded to me. Often while traveling abroad, we visited places of historic relevance, saw great works of art, and met dignitaries. Yet I know that my strongest desires to learn were a result of experiences shared with Mum, Mimi, Rie, and my Grandpapa.

I figured out the joy and science of cooking early on, making and baking cookies and crepes. I learned how to mix colors as I dabbed paint on my palette, creating my works of art, according to Rie.

Exploring the beach with my Grandpapa, I would discover the importance of tides rising and falling and how the sea's movement impacted the size of the moon. The more experiences that I had promoted my desire to learn.

One state that was instilled in me early on was to persevere when challenged. A competitive edge was encouraged, but only to spur on my efforts, even when presented with difficult tasks.

Clearly, my role models, Mum, Mimi, Rie, and Grandpapa persevered during events involving perils of war, traveling across the ocean to seek a new life, and when Mum and Mimi assumed full responsibility for me after all our great men passed away.

My family members taught me to take what I have learned to implement acquired skills and, most importantly, apply those skills.

There is no simple answer. I conclude and emphasize that each trait- one's quest to learn, perseverance to seek knowledge, and application- are equally important. That is my truth as I submit my answer. Your encouragement is greatly appreciated.

Sincerely,
Allie Reddinger

My confidence seemed to be growing, as I thought about all these aspects related to acquiring knowledge. Rie had an enormous influence on Mum, Mimi, and me. I stopped typing and held my locket, recalling the many experiences we shared.

Looking at the clock, I was surprised by the time. Most of my afternoon was spent composing my response. The beach was calling me, so I pulled on a hoodie and headed down the stairs.

Enticing aromas that wafted up through my grate now beckoning me into the kitchen where Mum and Mimi were baking. Each smiled at me as they kneaded and rolled the dough.

Mum handed me a roll and an apple, saying, "Dinner will be ready in an hour. Looks like you need some fresh air." Taking a bite, I nodded and off I went.

The sun was setting, and a few neighbors waved as I walked by. The cool wind and salt air refreshed my senses. *Most likely, I would hear back from the Academy the next morning unless I blew it.*

I could almost feel Rie's presence and her words whispering that *my truth would be acknowledged, and not to fret.*

Time to turn back as my stomach grumbled, indicating that I was hungry!

A mug of chowder awaited me along with some scrumptious French bread. Mum and Mimi awaited me, expecting an update.

"Well," I said, "I think that I am responding to the second challenge with honesty and common sense."

Both nodded and chuckled, "No doubt," Mum encouraged.

Since we ate late, I decided to head off to bed and read a new novel. After hugs and kisses, I scurried upstairs. I barely opened my book before I drifted off to sleep, snuggling my stuffie, Babbitt.

I woke to the sound of a doorbell. Running downstairs, I saw the postman handing Mimi another envelope. The postmark looked like the one sent previously from the Academy, yet it was still hard to determine the location of origin. Nervous, I went out on the porch, carefully opened it, and read.

March 9, 2022

Dear Ms. Reddinger,

Allie, the Council for BETA is pleased with your progress thus far. You have now completed half of the Key Challenges. Your imaginative nature has been observed by many. Your language development has been beyond reproach. Because you are an avid reader, your creativity and imagination have been greatly nurtured.

Members of the Academy were enthused by your belief in fairies, knowing that most thought they were only imaginary friends. We know better. As you can tell, we find imagination to be an important matter.

The Keys of Imagination are:
- *Creativity: Being Unique*
- *Fearless: Unlimited Thinking*
- *Curiosity: Inquisitiveness*

Allie, your challenge to acquire your third key will not present you with a trick, as the correct answer you will pick. Look deep in your heart and mind, and the correct answer you'll find.

The Council is rooting for you.
Sincerely and Best Wishes,

The Council for BETA

Opening my laptop, I went to my notes folder. *Halfway?* I thought. *Fairies?* I would need to think about that reference. Some of my artwork that I painted with Rie featured fairies. Perhaps as a child, I believed they were real.

As I considered this aspect, I went into the kitchen. Mum was there, and before she asked, I assured her, "Yes, I'm progressing."

"Great!" she responded.

Mum and Mimi never pried, and that attribute is one I most definitely appreciated.

Mum set down a peanut butter, banana, and yogurt smoothie along with a thick slice crust of buttered bread.

After I finished, I headed to Rie's library where I would compose my thoughts.

Being Unique…Is being a child prodigy unique? Maybe. I have been primarily raised by strong women, and all my significant family members are artists, so creativity is part of my uniqueness. My reading level is quite high too.

Being Fearless… Unlimited thinking. I am not easily swayed by others and think for myself. Often, we would debate topics, and I would state my position based on researched facts. With Grandpapa, we'd play games of strategy, like chess. All these endeavors heightened my critical thinking skills.

Being Curious… For sure, I excel in this area. My family members were plagued by my constant questions about what made the world tick. They all joked about how I would persist with questions about how things worked until my curiosity was satisfied.

Now I was ready to respond. Opening the site, I began my response.

March 10, 2022

Dear Council for BETA,

As a potential candidate for BETA membership, I recognize that these challenges are providing me with in- depth analysis of key traits for consideration. Throughout my almost twelve years of life, family members and significant people have often remarked on my keen imagination.

In some ways, it makes sense that I would be creative and unique. This statement is not intended to boast, but rather a reflection of my upbringing by artists. Rie was a designer in Paris, and met my Grandpapa, who was a renowned photographer.

Early on, I gained insights into fabrics, dyes, and the art of finding the perfect lighting to snap a photo. An easel was always available to me, allowing me to readily mixed colors on a palette and spend hours crafting distinctive pottery. Our kitchen, the greatest canvas of all, would often be covered in flour, and my fingers were sticky from hours baking bread and cookies. Not everyone my age can successfully bake a souffle.

I must confess that this challenge is providing me with unlimited opportunities to think critically and be fearless with my responses. Like the members of my family, I am an avid reader. They have encouraged me to explore and conduct research on various topics.

We often have debates grounded in facts, which have honed my analytical thinking and information processing skills. From an early age, my Grandpapa initiated games that required strategic thinking, like chess.

Almost to a fault, curiosity is a defining trait of mine. I am ever so curious. The beach, which is our backyard, serves as an extensive classroom where daily walks allow me with an opportunity to explore and expand my curiosity. I investigate how tides impact our coastline and why different bird species exhibit seasonal migratory patterns.

On our walks, my Grandpapa would pose questions, prompting me to head home to consult reference books in search of answers, always eager to learn something new. Most likely, I drove my family crazy by asking countless questions about almost any new experience I undertook. Their patience and willingness to invest time have been instrumental in fostering my curiosity and thirst for knowledge.

Once again, I know that I can find the correct answers. It is within my reach. I will look deep in my heart and mind, recognizing that creativity, fearlessness, and curiosity are all equally essential traits in responding to the Key Challenge of Imagination.

I appreciate that the Council for BETAs is rooting for me. My heart tells me that my answer is based on truth as I understand it.

Sincerely,
Allie Reddinger

I reviewed my response and pressed "Send." Perhaps the pace and introspection with each challenge was somewhat exhausting me. Some yoga might help relieve the stress.

I got out my mat, and Mum came out and asked to join me.

"Hey, sweet girl, can I join you?"

"Sure, Mum, that would be super!"

With our mats spread out, we stretched and then went through a routine of breathing, moving into warrior poses, then downward dog, and ending with a sun salutation.

"I am feeling great and hungry!" I told Mum.

Into the kitchen, I went, and there waiting for me was my favorite chicken marsala and homemade noodles. *"Delicious!"*

Mimi joined us at the table. I informed them of my progress without disclosing too much information.

"Only one challenge left, and due to the quickness of their responses, perhaps I will know soon whether or not I can attend the Academy! Fingers crossed!"

Mimi spoke up, sharing, "One day, you can elaborate about your efforts. Remember, Rie left some journals that she wrote about her attendance at the Academy; so if accepted, perhaps you might take a look."

"Sure, her notes might enlighten me," I said.

Upstairs, I took a long, hot bath. Feeling ever so relaxed, I fell asleep quickly.

The next morning, I could hear the howling winds. A storm was brewing. *Perhaps a premonition about the future?* I wondered. *No way*, I thought. Looking out from the balcony, I could see the postman approaching the house. *Always dependable, bad weather would not prevent their delivery.*

Before he arrived, I was waiting by the door. Mimi had bagged some freshly baked muffins, so as I reached for the envelope, I exchanged it for the goodie bag.

"Thanks, the muffins smell wonderful! Can't imagine what project you are working on, Allie. Have fun!" he said.

Thanking him, he left, and I took the envelope into the library. Anxious, I nestled into a comfy chaired, and opened it, and began to read.

March 11, 2022

Dear Ms. Reddinger,

Allie, The Council for BETA applauds you for reaching the final Key Challenge. Once you have completed your last task, the Council will inform you if you have been successful in earning each key.

Loyalty is a must-have trait for any and all BETAs. Reliable sources have shared that you are loyal friend to many pals and are also most loyal to your family.

The Keys of Loyalty are:
- *Faith: Allegiance*
- *Honesty: Truthfulness*
- *Support: Foundation*

Allie, as stated for each challenge, there is never a trick, when you pick the answer, look deep in your heart and mind, no doubt the correct answer you will find.

The Council will review all four Key Challenge responses you have provided. We hope to reward you with all four keys. Then, one more challenge will follow.

The Council is excited to review your response.

Sincerely and Best Wishes,

The Council for BETA

Finally, I was presented with my last challenge. Being faithful, honest and supportive makes sense. Loyalty would be an important trait for a BETA trainees. I realize that self-reflection has provided me with a positive opportunity and has been meaningful.

One point for me is remembering Rie and Grandpapa who were youngsters during World War II. They were faced with dangers, and being faithful and allegiant to their country was critical. Each had shared many perilous situations resulting from countrymen being disloyal to their country.

Being honest or truthful is a true test of valor. I never wanted to be disloyal to my family and friends.

As Rie stated, "One should always look in your heart and mind, and truth you will find."

My family always stressed the importance of honesty, and I would never lie and disappoint them.

Loyalty depends on bonding. You naturally bond with your family. But being loyal to friends is important, especially if they are bullied by others. I recall being loyal in times of need.

Our family depended on one another to bond and be ever so loyal when loved ones passed on. There was a lot of loss in our family.

I was a little nervous, but excited to draft my final response for the last Key Challenge. The Council for BETA had really encouraged me throughout this process, so I planned to respond with optimism.

I sat at my laptop, opened my folder and wrote.

March 12, 2022

Dear the Council for BETA,

As I respond to my final Key Challenge, I do so with excitement about my potential acceptance into the Academy. Perhaps the last key of being loyal is ever so significant since that trait would be critical for the success of one's overall ability. I agree with the Academy's review of my observable loyalty to friends and most importantly to my family.

I considered each key aspect of Loyalty, the first being allegiant or being faithful. The Academy is most aware of my heritage. My Great Grandmother Rie was a telepath. This incredible discovery was recently presented to me.

When she and my Grandpapa were young, they lived in both France and England during World War II. They each faced countrymen who were disloyal, and each experienced dangerous situations as a result. They stressed the importance of allegiance to their country and family.

Along with allegiance, one must be honest and truthful. Perhaps what they experienced at such an early age influenced how truth and honesty became an integral life value for them. Rie expressed in her message to me that if I looked into my heart and mind, truth I would always find. Good advice, I thought. That is the manner in which I have always approached all the key challenges. I would never disappoint my family and be dishonest.

One would expect that being faithful and honest would result in one's bonding and provide support. With friends, I have seen bullying, and I always tried to demonstrate traits composing all three aspects of loyalty. This has served me well and my family too.

After great thought, I submit that each key aspect of loyalty; being faithful, honest, and supportive are equally important. These challenges have offered me opportunities to reflect deeply and see the truth.

The Academy has never thought to trick and allowed me, with deep thought, to pick the correct answer, I infer. I look forward to receiving your response and to completing the final challenge prior to possible acceptance into the BETA.

With great appreciation for this opportunity,

Sincerely and Best Wishes,
Allie Redding

Taking in a deep breath after my final review, I pressed "send." Now I waited for the final response to find out if I would be given an opportunity to become a BETA trainee. After a delicious and satisfying meal, I headed to my room.

The stars were so bright as I peered through my telescope. Perhaps that was good sign. I fell asleep and dreamed.

During the night, Mum entered my room. Calling out, she gently shook me awake. My covers had tumbled onto the floor as I had been sweating profusely. Not remembering my dream exactly, there was a sense of darkness that appeared to overwhelm me.

Perhaps all the reflection and deep thinking had exhausted me, resulting in my bad dream. Mum cuddled with me, covering us as we both fell asleep.

The next morning, I woke up hoping to hear back from the Academy. Sunlight cast soft hues dancing across my ceiling. The scent of cinnamon wafted through my room from the kitchen below. Mum and Mimi greeted me with a plate of French toast drizzled with homemade syrup. Mimi gave me a big hug, and they both waited for me to speak.

With a smile, I said, "All's fine. I think I was so tired that my sleep patterns were off, so I had a dark dream, but I can't remember it."

I knew that I might later recall that conversation. My thoughts might run much deeper than I realized.

The postman came and went without a response from the Academy. Mum and Mimi reassured me that perhaps they needed to review all the information prior to sharing their recommendation.

They suggested that we take a short road trip into Charleston to shop and enjoy a late lunch on Rutledge Avenue. We all loved brunching out on the patio, savoring dishes like shrimp and cheese grits. After our delicious meal, we stopped and picked up bread and sweets to take home.

Later, Mum, Mimi, and I nibbled on bread, cheese, and pastries with some sweet tea. Full,, we retired early.

The doorbell woke me. Checking the time, I was surprised by how early it was. I threw on my sweats and hoodie, then rushed downstairs.

Our postman smiled as he handed me a thick envelope.

"Look, Allie, the postmark is now clear, and it's addressed from England!"

"Thanks! Mum, Mimi, the envelope is here, and it was sent from England!" I shouted.

I hurried into the kitchen and sat on a stool. Opening the envelope, I noticed a small packet enclosed with the letter.

Pulling out the letter, I read.

March 14, 2022

Dear Ms. Reddinger,

Allie, the Council for BETA has reviewed your answers to The 4 Key Challenges. We are pleased to inform you that you have responded correctly to each challenge. Your responses clearly demonstrate your understanding of key traits pertaining to Character, Knowledge, Imagination, and Loyalty.

You have earned four keys.

Now, one more challenge awaits you.

Enclosed, you will find a packet containing four door keys. You must select the right key to unlock and open the front door to the Academy for the BETA. Like the other challenges, there is no trick. Choose wisely and pick. This is the most important moment to look into your heart and mind and the correct door key you will find.

The Council believes in you and hopes that you will pick the key to open the Academy door. Once you enter, you will start your trainee journey to become a BETA.

Good luck and Best Wishes,
The Council for BETA

"Mum, Mimi!" I shouted.

They came running from the kitchen.

"Are you OK?" they asked. Mimi waited for my response.

"I made it! I will be accepted once I complete the last challenge. The Council believes that I answered all the Key Challenges! Now I need to head to the Academy take one of the four keys sent to me and open the front door into the Academy! Do either of you know where the Academy might be? Maybe France?"

I held my locket from Rie ever so tightly, remembering that she had attended the Academy so many years before.

"No, we will receive an email finalizing all the information." Mum replied.

While I waited, I chose to enter Rie's library. There I sensed her presence as well as Grandpapa's. The room was always warm and welcoming, filled with photos and paintings, as well as trinkets gathered throughout the years. Rie's desk was no longer locked, and her notes or letters were there for me. She had suggested waiting to delve too much into her probable attendance until I might undertake an adventure.

Mum popped her head in, and I asked, "Do you think that I can read some notes that Rie wrote about her journey? I won't read much, but just to get an idea."

Mum nodded in agreement and closed the door, leaving a cool beverage for me.

I opened Rie's desk drawer and pulled out the neatly bound notebook. A silk ribbon tied the contents securely. Rie's script neatly flowed across the page and looked very similar to letters written to me from her. The paper was refined, and it appeared that on the margins, she drew flowers. My emotions were running high as I read her first entry.

February 19, 1940

Dear Lovey,

Today was a very busy Monday in school. Our professors seemed to be focused on world affairs. My Papa, involved in our local government, discussed concerns about Germany and France's vulnerability. Today, like most days, I felt secure since I attended my school close to home. Some of my friends went to boarding schools in Switzerland. Just like today, I was happy to come home and share the events of my day. I heard some tapping on my door. "Entre." Mere and Papa entered. Papa was holding a thick envelope. Both asked about my day and then Papa told me about the content of the envelope. Looking at Mere, she seemed somewhat reticent. Papa shared that an Academy was inquiring about prospective trainees, and my name had been proposed by my école. He pulled out the paperwork, and I looked at the expansive documents. There was no mention of where the school was located. Papa said that no decision would be made right away, but we all might want to explore this option. I knew they were both concerned about a probable invasion by Germany. I told them both that I would look over the papers.

Looks like lots of information to gather. Not sure, Lovey, what I think about this.

My Deepest Thoughts,
Rie

Obviously, if Rie went to the Academy, as I imagined, her process was quite different from mine. My plan was to read a few more excerpts and find out more.

February 20, 1940

Dear Lovey,

 I got back from school, and today, many of my classmates were talking about possible future plans. I chose not to disclose that my family had been contacted by an Academy.

 I pulled out the documents and saw that the first part described my family background. Researching my ancestry, I learned that the DuBois family was affluent, and there was some aristocratic lineage, no royalty, but some connections. I may be a princess in my parents' eyes, but not in the DuBois legacy.

 My family history would be easy to write about. I also saw where my school records would be documented, and referrals from staff could be readily gathered. Appraisals from my community would also be sought to gain feedback, hopefully positive, I thought.

 The last section would be compiled by me. The section addressed four key areas. My essay would describe my beliefs regarding my Character, Knowledge, Imagination, and Loyalty. The Academy reminded me that this process was not set to trick, and truthful responses would be there for me to pick.

 Naturally, I enjoyed the challenge, and this process could be worth trying. I would tell Mere and Papa that I would accept the process and see if I am a worthy candidate for the Academy.

 My Deepest Thoughts,
 Rie

Odd, I thought. Rie had to complete an essay; however, the challenges were similar. Perhaps due to the perilous times, timelines were constrained. I planned to read one more entry.

February 21, 1940

Dear Lovey,

Being introduced to this process intrigued me. After all, I had always been curious about a fault. Mulling over ideas, I started considering each topic and did outlines. Immersed in my work, I barely heard the tap on my door.

Papa entered and informed me that later that afternoon, two professors from the Academy would visit us. Ms. Beatty and Mr. Finney would be here for a visit. Mere was preparing an afternoon tea with cheeses, fruit, and pastries. I chose to change from my school uniform and dressed in a sweater and plaid skirt, wearing my favorite boots. Mere approved, and nervously I waited, and then the bell rang.

Mr. Finney's brogue seemed Irish, and he had a twinkle in his eye. Ms. Beatty was dressed in vivid colors with a knitted shawl draped over her shoulders. She had a great and welcoming smile. I Loved her silver and gemmed jewelry. She was so stylish, and there was a hint of an Irish accent.

Mere seemed comfortable, and my confidence heightened as we chatted. Maybe, if accepted, the Academy might be the place for me. I was grateful for their encouragement.

My Deepest Thoughts,
Rie

Based on my readings, I clutched my locket and definitely felt Rie's presence. This amount of information that I gleaned from her diary allowed me to see some similarities about attending the Academy.

As Rie suggested, I would hold off any further review until, if I attended the Academy, and then I could learn more about her experience. That was what she suggested, and I knew that was the appropriate decision.

Later that day, Mum received an email disclosing the destination was England, and since our passports were current, tickets would be available at the Atlanta airport.

Mum suggested that, based on their recommendations, I should pack for a few weeks as that would be sufficient for an extended stay. "Wow! Now I knew that the B in BETA stood for British, so off to London we'd head."

Excited, I told Mum, "I am so excited knowing where I might be attending school."

I hurried upstairs and organized my clothing and supplies as suggested. Sitting on my bed, I fiddled with Rie's locket, imagining how she must have felt so many years before. As I worked through my challenges, I felt her presence seeking truth as I did.

The next day we uploaded all my technology, getting phone and iPad chargers. We would leave the following morning. My luggage was in front of the door, as was Babbitt, my rabbit stuffy, a gift from Rie and Grandpapa from an early age. Aside from my photos and locket, Babbitt was my main connection to home.

The next morning, our departure date arrived and, not feeling hungry, I nibbled on a protein bar. Before eight, we took a short ride to Charleston airport and then flew to Atlanta, from where we would jet off to London. I was somewhat nervous, yet excited, too! I had only read a few excerpts from Rie's diary since her birthday letter suggested that I wait and experience my own possible journey first.

As she stated in her letter, *"I would most certainly partake in an amazing adventure of my lifetime!"* Mum and Mimi, as expected, were all smiles and gave me plenty of hugs. Relieved, they both would be close by when I began my session if accepted, and calls could occur nightly.

We arrived in England that night. After a day to unwind, we would be picked up by the Academy limousine and whisked off to school.

The night of our arrival, I was restless and dreamed about Rie. My dream was so comforting since Rie and I were in her library, and she was sharing experiences from her childhood at her family's country estate outside of Paris. My anxiety eased as I could hear her soft and comforting voice.

Waking up early, I recognized my stuffie and decided to take a walk in a nearby park to clear my mind. An early walk reminded me of many occasions walking on the beach with Grandpapa. Mum, Mimi, and I enjoyed afternoon tea and looked forward to checking out the Academy the next day.

I slept better and once again woke before the sun rose. Mum was awake, and I went in and cuddled with her.

"Mimi and I are excited for you, Allie, and I look forward to hearing all about your journey. As Rie said, you will find the truth about yourself and about her too. We'll be here for a short time, and when we leave, you can reach us daily. Love you so much."

"Love you both bunches!" I hugged her tightly.

Mimi joined us, and we ate a light breakfast. She too shared her confidence in me, and then there was a tap on the door.

A tall gentleman greeted Mum. He had a city or cockney accent, and his grin was welcoming. "Hello, Mrs. Reddinger, I am Mr. Berry from the Academy. I am here to pick up Allie and you both to go out to the Academy."

After putting my luggage into the shiny limo, I sat in between Mum and Mimi, hugging Babbitt. The day was sunny and cool as we drove through London heading out into the countryside.

I had visited years before, so I was somewhat comforted by the familiarity. "*I wondered if the Academy would be in a castle surrounded by a moat,*" but I chuckled at my silly thought.

Soon, we drove up a winding road and stopped before a tall wrought-iron fenced gate. Mr. Berry pressed a button, and the gate swung open as we drove up to a large estate surrounded by massive trees graced by gardens.

My nerves were settling down. The lovely old estate reminded me of charming southern estates familiar to me. *"The Academy looked promising. One more challenge left."*

The limo stopped in front of a stairway leading to the sturdy massive door. I fumbled in my pocket and picked out one of my four keys, hearing Rie's words, *"Truth you will find."*

The Academy had advised me throughout my journey, *"that there was no trick, the correct answer I would pick!"* I held the key out and, said to myself, *"Let's see if I chose the correct key."*

I shrugged my shoulders and smiling slightly, then placed the key in the lock and turned.

THE ACADEMY: BETA

CLICK! THE DOOR UNLOCKED AS I TURNED THE KNOB. I sighed and took a deep breath overcome with relief. Mum and Mimi followed me in, patting me on the back.

Standing at the entryway were two striking adults. A tall woman smiled and spoke with a slight Irish accent.

"Welcome, Allie, Mrs. Reddinger, and Madam. I am Ms. Beatty, an instructor."

She wore a long denim skirt, and a silk shirt covered by a brightly hued poncho. I was struck by her silver pendant and wide leather belt adorned with turquoise stones. Looking down, I could see that her skirt fell above some exquisite suede boots. *"My Rie, who designed fashion, would love her attire."*

Mr. Dunbar was also noticeable. When he spoke, you thought he was from British aristocracy, reminding me of Grandpapa.

"Hi, Allie and Madams. As Ms. Beatty stated, we are looking forward to our journey with you at the Academy. We will be your instructors and mentors. Later, you will meet Mr. Finney."

His reddish-brown hair curled down to his collar of a white, soft shirt with full sleeves looking as if he might pull out a sword from a waistcoat and shout, *"En Garde!"*

Both he and Ms. Beatty grinned, making me wonder if they were reading my mind since they were most likely telepathic. Surely that would be a skill I would need to work on here.

The entryway was spectacular, with polished floors, plush chairs, and sofas. An incredible staircase with a curved railing led to the upstairs dorms. Before Mum and Mimi left, we had a spot of tea in the small, elegant tearoom and then they walked up the stairs to my room.

Ms. Beatty explained, "While the dorms are on the second floor, the classrooms are in a separate area. Tomorrow, you will get a tour with your fellow classmates and see the grounds, which include several acres.

Don't worry, Madams; there is considerable security! I thought Ms. Beatty was reading Mum and Mimi's minds about safety.

I arrived at a lovely room with lots of natural light and noticed two beds.

"Wow! I'm looking forward to having a roommate!" I exclaimed.

Ms. Beatty smiled and said, "Yes, she'll arrive soon, and you will have a suitemate too."

I bid farewell to Mum and Mimi, and they said they would call me later. The room was airy, with tall and deep windows that allowed light to filter in, much to my liking. Perhaps I would turn my bed around so I would wake, like I did at home, as the morning sun rose.

I decided to wait until my roomie arrived before I unpacked to see which bed and closet she'd prefer.

Out in the hall, I heard a hearty laugh. Then a tall, lovely girl popped her head into the room. She was accompanied by a short, cheerful-looking woman and a little gal who was the exact image of her apparent sister.

"Thanks, Mr. Berry, for carrying my stuff. I see my roommate is inside, so I will say hello."

KIT MCLEAN

KIT PEERED INTO THE ROOM. SHE WAS TALL AND WILLOWY. The light accentuated her porcelain skin tone, and alabaster wavy hair fell to her shoulders. What was most striking was her violet eyes.

Smiling, she said, "Hi, Allie, Mr. Berry told me who my roomie was. This is my little sis, Becky, and my Aunt Tessie."

Aunt Tessie spoke up, "Hello, Allie, we McLeans are Gaelic and not the typical red-headed, green-eyed Irish. Our heritage consists of tall, dark-haired lads and lasses with violet eyes. We met your Mum and Mimi as we arrived. Kit and Becky are visiting me while their parents are searching for antiquities."

Chiming in, Kit shared, "Actually, we live in Dublin, Georgia."

"Actually, I live close to you, near Charleston, South Carolina," Allie said.

Aunt Tessie told Becky that it was time to go and told Kit that her parents would call her later. Becky squeezed Kit tightly, as Kit patted her on the head and kissed her. Now we were together, and I asked," Which side do you want to sleep on?"

Kit laughed and said, "We Gaels prefer the right side nearest the door. Tales shared from the past suggest that if a tricky situation presents itself, then one can escape if need be! Perhaps we Gaels are somewhat superstitious!" Kit belly laughed, and I giggled with her. I figured that we'd be a great pair.

She continued, "Most of my family were born and lived in Ireland. For centuries, they were known as treasure hunters and made great discoveries, finding heirlooms belonging to many kingdoms. Rumors were that they could travel through times as transporters. Yes, I can transport, but my skills are shaky." "*Sounds like me, I thought.*"

"Your background is amazing! I have read about time travel and watched movies and wondered if that was possible! Wow! Incredible!" I exclaimed.

"I am somewhat telepathic. My Great-grandmother Rie was one, and I just learned that she also attended the Academy almost a century before. You'll see when I share some of her photos that I favor her, being fair, blonde, and having hazel eyes. When she was alive, I recall her taking time with me since sometimes I experienced head noises, and she and I would practice yoga and we would breathe together."

Then I showed Kit my locket. "Rie wrote me a letter many years ago, and in it, she told me that I would go on a journey, which brought me here. I received the letter along with my locket. As you can see, her message to look in my heart and mind and truth I will find is so encouraging."

Kit smiled as she gazed at the script and said, "Intriguing and at the same time so thoughtful and lovely!"

Resuming my story, "Rie lived in France and was selected to attend during World War II. While here she wrote diaries and journals that I've barely started and will get to read later once I finish training. Like you, my rusty telepathic skills will improve."

Then I told her about how my Rie met Grandpapa. "I'm sure she shared her experiences during the war, and he knew about her telepathic abilities. She channeled her artistic skills, and he became a famous photographer. Each relayed the perilous challenges of living during World War II and how they and their families survived. I will find out more about those days since she attended the Academy during the same time period."

Kit listened attentively and said, "Allie, your family story is incredible, and your Great Grandparents experienced such a romantic love story. I wonder if somehow I too and my family are connected to the Academy. I believe that I possess some telepathic abilities since I see pictures in my head. I never thought much about it until now! Can't wait to meet our other classmates."

"Me too," I agreed.

CHRISTAN CHAN

KIT AND I SAT ON OUR BEDS, LISTENING FOR FOOTSTEPS AND ANTICIPATING OTHER ARRIVALS. Further down the hallway, we heard some chatter. A few minutes later, a rather tall young man tapped on our door and stepped in.

"Hi, I'm Christan Chan. My room is down the hall, and I am waiting for my roomie."

"Come on in," Kit said.

Christan was dressed in jeans, a T-shirt, and a hoodie. His hair was a shiny black mop, while his eyes were dark. He had the most appealing smile and a charming British accent. Kit and I introduced ourselves.

"So what's your story?" Kit boldly asked.

Grinning, he sat on the edge of my bed and began.

"Currently, I live here in London. The Chan family might have a connection to the Academy. We have a long history as healers. My parents are both Asian and Afrikaner. They met in school as psychology majors. Perhaps it is a given with my genetic makeup that I have some abilities in reading body language and emotions.

Like you two, I am considered to be a bright twelve-year-old. I am guessing that you both are exceptional and are attending the Academy for that reason. I will have fun with others who share similar skills, especially since I am an only child."

"Me too," I chimed in.

Continuing, he shared, "My family has traveled quite a bit, but now their practice is here in London. I am sure more will be shared about each of us, but fill me in, you two."

Kit started and did her best to imitate a Gaelic accent while sharing her family history. She mentioned that her parents sought antiquities and could teleport. Christan smiled and laughed as she embellished her family history.

He looked somewhat surprised when I showed him my locket and explained that I too, like Rie, was telepathic, and she had been a trainee at the Academy.

AIDEN AND AMAYA SONG

WE HEARD CHATTER IN THE HALL. IT SOUNDED LIKE TWO OTHERS WERE TALKING TO MR. BERRY. Mr. Berry stated that Aiden would share his room with Christan, and Amaya would be housed in the suite next to Kit and me.

Christan called out, "Hello, you two, come and meet our fellow trainees."

A girl and a boy of approximately the same height entered.

"Hi, I am Aiden, and this is my sister, Amaya Song. Obviously, we are fraternal twins."

Aiden and Amaya were of Asian descent, with dark, silky hair, and oddly, each had different colored eyes; blue and green. *"I guessed I would be the blonde in the group."*

Aiden spoke up, "By about thirty minutes, I am the oldest!"

"Yes," agreed Amaya, "but I am the sharpest!" Amaya grinned and poked Aiden. She was ecstatic that she was sharing a suite with us, and Aiden declared, "I am thrilled to hang out with another guy!"

Being the oldest, Aiden felt he should share most of the family history, "The Song family has a legacy as Meta- Physicists and

Scientists. They have documented inventions that benefit time travel and transport, dealing with the physics of energy, fire, ice, and water. Our family has some connection with the Academy, as I guess we all do. Right now, our family resides in California, and our parents work for an Institute. We have been evaluated within the top two percent of the intellectually gifted, and I imagine you all are too. Both of us possess abilities to transform fire and water, incorporating metaphysical skills. We have only had a few experiences using our abilities and depend on our ability to be connected to each other."

"Our twinness is so critical to how we function," declared Amaya. The three of us looked astonished by their claims.

Christan must have picked up on our thoughts. "I imagine as we discover more about ourselves, we will learn much from one another. Exploring our family connection and connection to the Academy will be cool," while nodding his head.

Now it was our turn to share our brief family review while the twins listened intently. They were both curious about our connections to the Academy. Kit enjoyed another opportunity to mimic her accent and share more tales about her parent's ability to transport and locate treasures.

Briefly and somewhat measured, I relayed Rie's history during World War II at the Academy and that I, like her, was telepathic. Aiden and Amaya were somewhat stunned by our backgrounds and keenly interested in Christan's knowledge of psychology.

Soon, Mr. Berry appeared. We guessed that he had other roles than being a chauffeur. Dinner was being served, so we all filed down to a large dining area with bright carpet and colorful art on the walls.

The food smelled good, and there was a variety of kid-friendly choices. Surprisingly, I was quite hungry and filled my plate with salad and tacos. There was an ice cream bar that enticed us to make sundaes.

Ms. Beatty and Mr. Dunbar joined us, and we had a lively discussion about local sports. We all knew how passionate the Brits were about soccer. Our instructors informed us that we were to convene in the small study after dinner.

THE ACADEMY'S HISTORY

MR. DUNBAR WAS SITTING IN A CHAIR IN FRONT OF A CIRCLE OF SEATS, FROM WHICH WE EACH CHOSE ONE. "Welcome to each of you. The Academy was pleased that you agreed to work on the Key challenges and were successful in completing one of each one, resulting in receiving four keys and selecting the correct key to open the door and enter the Academy. Now you will begin an amazing journey."

I thought about Rie's birthday letter, and she stated that soon I would go on an amazing journey, and she was right.

"I imagine that you were surprised to learn that the Academy was in England. Due to the privacy and focus of the training, we don't disclose the location until acceptance is apparent.

BETA represents the lowercase "b" of the Greek alphabet, signifies high energy, and stands for the "British Exceptional Training Academy.

The Academy did not disclose the location until the completion of the initial challenge. There are precautions for both the privacy and protection of the trainees.

More than a hundred years before, European countries were experiencing unrest, with a possible war looming. A group of scholars convened to gather a group of exceptionally bright students who exhibited unique skills.

The Academy was then formed with a specific Manual developed to describe the mission and training of each trainee. World War I happened, and the Academy was able to train students who could give back to society.

Somehow, the Key Training Manual was lost or possibly stolen. Now, Kit, this is where your family enters the Academy's history. As treasure hunters, who could transport and travel in time, your family located the Manual and returned it to the Facility. The Council requested that a member of the McLean family join the faculty. Relieved with the Manual returned, the Academy was able to train future *BETAS*.

In the 1930s, Europe again was faced with a possible war far more serious than World War I.

As you will discover, the Chan, Song, and DuBois families would complete The 4 Key Challenges and attend the Academy. Due to their incredible abilities and important heritage, the Academy offered refuge to them during these dangerous times.

Another trainee named Serge, was Slavic and part of a noble family who contributed greatly to the welfare of their country. Though his character was dubious, the Academy accepted him, urged by his family in the hope of some positive transformation.

Being able to transport and disguise, he posed a danger to the other trainees and especially to Rie. He also tried to steal the Manual. At times, the Academy suspected that Serge would interfere with the Academy's work and at times stoke fear in trainees; therefore, the Council expelled him.

Not to scare you, but learning about the history is relevant, and you will each spend more time discerning information about your legacy. Tomorrow you will receive your schedules and tour the school and grounds. Good night and sleep well."

Exhausted, we headed to our rooms. Our minds were filled with so much information, and in mine, so many unanswered questions.

DREAMS

UPSTAIRS IN OUR ROOMS, WE CHANGED INTO OUR PJ'S. Hugging and cuddling with babbitt, I looked over at Kit, who squeezed her stuffy cat, Scot. "My brain is fried, "I said.

"Mine too," sighed Kit.

I started to doze off and thought I heard Rie call me. The fog was all around me, pulling me down into the mire. *"Help me, Rie!"* I shouted. *"Help me!"*

"Allie, Allie, wake up!" I felt someone shaking me.

Opening my eyes, I saw Kit looking distraught. "Wake up, Allie, you must be dreaming."

My covers were on the floor, and my brow was filled with sweat. "Guess I was so tired that I had a bad dream. I'm OK," I grimaced. I tightly snuggled with Babbitt and fell back to sleep.

Amaya was standing over me when I woke. She was wearing a fuzzy hoodie with ears and furry slippers, looking like some kind of animal that escaped from the zoo.

After my restless night, I was happy to see her, and her big grin made me smile.

"Are you okay?" she questioned. "I thought I heard you calling out last night."

I vaguely remembered Kit shaking me awake from my dream. Sometimes I would dream deeply, not call them nightmares, but feelings of uncertainty and even sadness.

I had spoken to Mum and Mimi last night, but perhaps being away from family and the revelation of my heritage stirred up some memories.

"I'm fine. As a little girl, I would have bad dreams sometimes. There were times that I wondered if the dreams might be a premonition. Prior to coming here, I had a strange dream about my attendance, and Rie was ever so present. She might be sending me messages from the beyond" I giggled.

Anxiety crept into my deep thoughts, recalling the time I got lost from my Grandpapa on the beach during bad weather. It was very foggy that day.

"All's well," I professed.

Kit prompted us, saying, "We have 20 minutes to change, so hurry up, gals."

We dressed in shirts with the BETA insignia and donned pants, determined to look appropriate for school, and headed down to breakfast.

Aiden and Christan were already there, and when Christan gave me a wink, my heart fluttered some.

Kit poked me and whispered, "Your cheeks are pink."

After breakfast, we moved back to the small study. Mr. Dunbar was now seated with Ms. Beatty and introduced a Mr. Finney, obviously Irish. Mr. Dunbar began...

"I hope you all slept well. Let me introduce Mr. Finney, who will be one of your instructors. He, along with Ms. Beatty and I, will provide much of your training. Right now, we will review your pledge and then discuss some important information. You'll receive your schedule, and a tour will occur. First, we will read your pledge that you will date and sign. All trainees are expected to sign the pledge. The *BETA* pledge is as follows."

BETA Pledge

I, Allie Reddinger,
Hereby agree to uphold each trait under the
Key of Character
Key of Knowledge
Key of Imagination
And,
Key of Loyalty
My loyalty will be demonstrated by following all rules and expectations,
As well as supporting my fellow Trainees, and
Maintaining the Academy's privacy.

Signed: ARed
Date: March 18, 2022

"One more area that we will need to discuss with each of you. You all have significant connections to the Academy. Over time, you will learn more about your roots. Throughout your training, as you develop skills and improve upon those you possess, you will become more confident. Overcoming your fears is equally important. Ms. Beatty will now take over this discussion."

I noticed Ms. Beatty was dressed in a long silk forest green shirt dress that grazed her ankles. Gold hoops dangled from her ears and could barely be seen in her thick mane of chestnut hair. Several gold chains hung around her neck. Her leather boots matched her dress. *All the councilors were well-dressed, for sure*, I thought. Ms. Beatty clasped her hands, speaking in a gentle tone.

FEARS

"I ASSURE YOU THAT ALL OF US EXPERIENCE FEARS AT SOME POINT IN OUR LIVES. When we are small, we can fear the unknown as we start to walk and talk. Going to school and meeting new people present us with small and sometimes large moments of uncertainty, but each of these fears shouldn't paralyze you and ultimately interfere in your progress."

I looked around and noticed Aiden and Christan sinking back in their chairs while Amaya, Kit, and I squirmed some.

"You each will become more self-assured over the next couple of weeks and months of your training, but we believe each of you needs to confront your fears. Talking about your fears is a positive strategy. Not to embarrass you, but we believe expressing the fears that are most relevant to you allows each one to progress here at the Academy."

Time for disclosure, I thought. *Seemed like group therapy.*

I raised my hand and declared, "I don't mind sharing."

"Go ahead, Allie."

Sensing her encouragement, I began...

"I live at the beach in South Carolina. Sometimes, the fog will roll in from the ocean, especially when storms threaten the area. My Mum, Mimi, Rie, and Grandpapa lived together in our cottage by the seaside. Grandpapa and I often would walk along the beach, taking photos and finding seashells. One day, when I was five, I walked away from Grandpapa far up on the beach when the fog started to drift in, and swiftly blocked me from his sight. I could only hear the waves crashing but not him calling me. I sat down, fearing that the fog would swallow me and toss me into the ocean. As I sat crying, Grandpapa located me. I was cold and shaking. Later, he and Rie gave me tips about what to do if I became lost in a foggy area. One important strategy was to keep an eye on the weather. If disoriented, try to look for a familiar sight and listen carefully to the noise around me. Yet soon thereafter, I experienced bad dreams about being lost in the fog. Sometimes, I would call out, and Rie would come into my room and cuddle me. For some reason, I often dreamt about the fog, and both Rie and I were swallowed by the mist together.

When I shared my dream with her, Rie tried not to express any emotions. Perhaps through our telepathic connection, she too had a bad experience, and I might have relived it in my dreams. Now I know more about her dangerous times during the war that could explain some of our shared emotions and connections. I had a scary experience, and Rie had one too. If I woke up tense, we would paint and do yoga to alleviate my stress."

Shrugging her shoulders, Kit began

"You all know that the Mclean family was involved with the Academy whence it started. As was shared with us, the Academy Manual was stolen, and my family recovered it. Obviously, like you, I just found out about this feat and the implications. We Gaels often boast and share myth and lore about time travel, and at times, I thought it was another Gaelic fable. I never knew the extent of their abilities.

Our family are treasure hunters and are now more involved in finding heirlooms. Yes, they would transport and travel through time. I have been able to transport some, but I am a novice. My greatest fear is that my parents will transport me and get lost and not return home, and that could also happen to me or my little sis. My family has explained how they are able to move through space and time without getting stuck or lost. My parents believe that my attendance at the Academy will allow me to develop skills and overcome my fears," I gave her a pat and a reassuring smile.

Christan now spoke up.

"My family lives in London. Being the son of psychologists can be interesting. Sometimes I feel that I am being observed and assessed, but they are loving and supportive.

My mother is an Afrikaner of European descent. She grew up in South Africa and moved to London as a child, attending school there. When she received her doctorate, she became a professor of psychology and soon thereafter met my father, and they opened their practice. On my father's side, they are of Chinese origin and have a long history of meditation and healing. When I was quite young, we traveled to China, where my grandfather wanted me to see the Great Wall of China As you all know, the wall is incredibly long and high. The amazing aspect is how it was constructed.

While there, one of my cousins dared me to climb up on the ledge, and I did. When I looked down, I became paralyzed with fear and thought I might tumble down.

My Grandfather, ever so wise, comforted me, telling me to focus and coaching me off the wall. I knew by his stern but calm expression, never to attempt that feat again. From that time forward, I try to avoid high places. Tall glass elevators and bridges are a little scary, and silly as it might seem, I don't generally climb trees. Might sound funny for a boy, but that's my story."

Shaking his head in agreement, Aiden concurred. "I don't like heights much either, Christan!"

Ms. Beatty encouraged Aiden to share his fears, and he readily did so.

"As you have observed, Amaya and I are fraternal twins. Twins possess special connectivity, sometimes called "Twinness."

"Yes," chimed in Amaya.

"We are hooked to the hip!" Aiden continued, and Amaya nodded in agreement."

"Although we are not identical, we still have amazing ways to sense each other even when we are not in the same area. Each of us appears to have been born with some metaphysical abilities that involve fire and water. Those skills we use with great caution. Most of all, I am sure Amaya would agree that we fear an inability to be connected. That phenomenon has occurred before when we are underground or separated by a distance. For example, one time, both of us were visiting caves, got lost, and we couldn't connect. Needless to say, we were located, and all was fine."

Amaya shook her head in agreement, saying, "That fear is powerful, so we try to plan ahead if we end up in unfamiliar spots."

I thought that Aiden was the dominant twin, maybe because he was born first. It will be very interesting to watch their interactions.

Aiden added, "Our other abilities, fire and water, are new to us. In times of stress, they can be a bit erratic if emotions gauge the outcome. We hope to rein in those skills and understand when it's appropriate to use them." Aiden concluded.

Then Ms. Beatty remarked in earnest, "Thank you, for sharing your personal fears. I am sure that might be the first time since most of this information is confidential. As your time here continues, you'll understand how significant having a peer group will be."

Looking around, I could tell that the information disclosed by one another astounded us. Perhaps we all were thinking about the intense journey we faced, but with excitement. My thoughts drifted to my Great Grandmother Rie. Holding my locket, I questioned.... *"Did she experience similar fears?"* Yes, I need to find the truth for sure...

Ms. Beatty smiled at me. *"Was she reading my mind?"*

"Thanks you for being so open and honest. I am excited to see that each of you is more aware of your fears. Note that some fears are similar between you, and some are not. Now we'll have a break and a snack. Afterward, we will head to the classroom for your schedule and take a tour. Hungry? See you all back in an hour."

All of us remained quiet as we entered the cafeteria. We now knew that each of us possessed unique qualities that would be revealed to one another in due course. *"I don't think any of us would have imagined this!"*

Loading our trays, we looked around, and Christan exclaimed, "Lots to work on, it might take a lifetime!" Giggling, we all nodded in agreement.

SCHOOL

FULLY SATISFIED AND OUR HUNGER ABATED, WE HEADED TO OUR CLASSROOMS. Though they were small, they were technologically rich, and we looked around in awe. Each student desk was equipped with a laptop, and there was also a smart board and an iPad available. Natural light filtered through the windows, offering views of the massive grounds. The soft green and blue hues provided a relaxed atmosphere, which I'm sure we'd appreciate as we anticipated the intense academic journey that awaited us. Mr. Dunbar, Ms. Beatty, and Mr. Finnegan were all seated in comfortable chairs and had pulled out five more in a semicircle.

Turning on our laptops, our *"menu"* appeared, and we scrolled down to the category, *"Classes."*

Mr. Dunbar spoke and shared, "These are your core areas of study. You will discover that each will overlap and build upon skills you will need as you delve into key aspects of each area."

"As you recall," Ms. Beatty added, "each of you completed the Key Challenge of Knowledge, demonstrating your quest for learning, perseverance, and the application of skills learned. As you work independently and together, you'll discover how your personal experiences contributes to your training."

"Now, please check out your classes and let us know if you have any questions," Mr. Finney concluded.

Core Classes:
- *Psychology*
- *Meditation*
- *Physics*
- *Telekinesis*
- *Linguistics*
- *Lip reading*
- *Chemistry*

We glanced at one another, and Christan winked at me. *These classes are intense*, I thought.

Psychology has always intrigued me, and I imagined that Christan would be a great source of knowledge since his parents are professionals. An area that I understand is meditation, as Rie and I often ended our yoga sessions in a calm and relaxed state of mind. Meditation can help you focus. I wonder if the others have tried it as well. Telekinesis is understandably a study that is unproven in terms of moving an object in space. However, Kit and her family can transport, so that must account for this area of study. It sounds scary but exciting too. Physics allows for the study of the natural science of matter, dealing with the movement and behavior of space and time. Naturally, I see the cumulative aspects of our classes relating to transporting, etc. Linguistics is critical for understanding the nuances of written and spoken communication and can greatly benefit our telepathic abilities. As for lipreading, I have spoken to individuals who are deaf, and they explain that this skill is difficult since many sounds and words look the same when spoken, but it can be taught. I've read many books about spies and wondered if Rie received training in all these areas during her time at the Academy in the War. "Did she receive training in all these areas?"

Chemistry rounds out the study of the properties and behavior of matter. Thinking this through, all these classes make sense to me, as each will provide us a direct path to understanding our abilities and allow for further development.

Taking in a deep breath, all of us knew we were in for an extensive journey to become *BETAs*.

All three instructors stood, and we completed the school tour. On the ground floor was a laboratory, and throughout the area were cozy, intimate study rooms. A map was displayed, and then as we moved out into the hallway, we noticed a massive wood-carved door. Mr. Dunbar opened the door with a key, and I was stunned by the walls and shelves lined with books from floor to ceiling. There were worn-leather and overstuffed chaise chairs, along with comfortable sofas. I was struck by the character of the room and the traditional feeling right at home since this library reminded me of mine at home. In the middle, on a mahogany-carved table, sat a large book under a dome.

Mr. Finney inserted a key, and we could now see the leather-bound book with a gilded title, *"BETA Manual."* Carefully, he opened it, and we saw aged parchment paper with a table of contents.

"Fellow Trainees, this Manual is your guide providing key information about your past, present, and future. When you enter the Library, you need to use your key to unlock the room and use a special key if you choose to explore information within the Manuel. The Library and the books within are always available to you. We have shared with you about the Academy's history and the attempt to steal the Manual. That explains why the room is locked, and we keep our guide under a protective dome. There you will find more information about your legacy."

Now a habit formed; I clutched my locket, feeling Rie's presence. Being the last to leave, I touched the Manual and felt a warm sensation. *"Did I imagine that?"* Only time would tell.

After a quick supper, I called Mum and Mimi. I decided not to share my dream and focused on my new friends, the modern classrooms, and the instructors.

"Mum, Mimi, I feel so comfortable here knowing that Rie attended so many years before. Each *BETA* has a connection too. I will call you tomorrow after classes begin. Night! Love you!" I ended my call, knowing that they felt more at ease with me so far away from home. As soon as my head hit the pillow, I fell asleep.

When I woke, Amaya and Kit were sitting on the bed.

"Whew," exclaimed Kit, "You slept soundly; you snored!"

I felt relieved; no bad dreams. I threw my pillow at her and jumped out of bed. After a quick shower, I pulled on my *BETA* hoodie, slacks, and Vans. Once downstairs, we met Christan and Aiden in the dining room. Hungry, I consumed an omelet, two slices of toast, and a glass of orange juice. We each grabbed water and some fruit as we walked to our classroom.

Mr. Dunbar sat while Mr. Finney stood by a model of the brain. "The brain had always intrigued me, given how much about its function remained a mystery."

Mr. Finney cleared his throat, capturing our attention. "I wondered if he was reading minds" when he stated, "Much about the brain remains unknown, but what we do know, we will apply to our training. Earlier, we brought up how each of you will employ key aspects related to each challenge. You all shared your understanding of the key components of "Knowledge," and your "Imagination" is equally relevant. The other two key areas, "Loyalty" and "Character," will also be significant as you move forward. Now, back to the brain." Mr. Dunbar took over. "Open your laptops, and you will see a diagram of the brain and a description of its purpose and function. The brain is a complex organ that controls thought, memory, emotion, touch, motor skills, vision, breathing, temperature, and every process that regulates how you process information and function. The diagram and explanation should be used as a source of reference. You will learn to control your thoughts, emotions, and breathing. Not so easy for twelve-year -olds to do, but you will learn these strategies and applying these techniques over time. Any questions?"

Mr. Dunbar concluded his initial presentation. The room was thick with silence, and no one looked at each other, trying to digest the intensity of the subject matter.

"Let's get started," Mr. Dunbar expressed with enthusiasm. "Christan, we know your parents are psychologists and most likely, as you shared, are the subject of tests and various programs that they have supervised." Christan nodded in agreement. Continuing, "Perhaps you have acquired a few techniques regarding body language."

Nodding again, Mr. Dunbar continued, "As you know, words matter; however, your first form of communication is nonverbal. We plan to spend today and tomorrow reviewing this area, knowing that we will build on these acquired skills throughout your training."

Now, Mr. Finney chimed in. "Eye contact and facial and body movement are what you see first. If one avoids eye contact when communicating, that might convey deception. The person might not smile. Nervous habits could be evident, like fidgeting, biting, scratching, and yes, sometimes hair standing on end! Most likely, they will not get that close to you."

I looked around, *wondering if anyone else had seen hair standing on end. Figure that.*

Clearing his throat, Mr. Finney continued, "They say that eyes are the windows to the soul. Now, in addition to the eyes, check out the mouth. One might grimace or twitch. Biting the inside of the mouth could be noticed. Pulling on the hair and sweating are possible behaviors to observe. Where are their hands? Are they holding them out, inside their pockets, or behind their back? Some may invade your personal space or choose to avoid it altogether. There's a lot to think about. Now we will show you some photos, and you will mark your sheets as "yes, dangerous" or "not." Then, you'll receive a percentage and some feedback. We will start slow and then pick up speed. Ready?"

The first was obvious, and then it became more difficult. "I bet Christan was sailing along," so I decided not to look over his way and really concentrated. The pressure was on, and my anxiety mounted. I hoped that Mr. Dunbar and Mr. Finney would share our scores in private.

"Time!" Mr. Dunbar called. "Your scores will only appear to you."

When my score popped up, *85%,* I was relieved. Mr. Finney walked by and said, "Good job!" Hopefully, I will improve my score the next time.

Our morning moved on quickly into mid- afternoon without a lunch break; however, we grabbed a snack to nourish our brains.

Mr. Dunbar dismissed class by saying, "You each have worked extra hard, so class is over for today. Go get some fresh air and review your notes for tomorrow. I'll see you bright and early. We have a surprise we will share with you tomorrow."

We all grabbed a quick snack and sat on the patio. Seeing the bikes, we each selected a helmet. Mr. Berry had informed us earlier that if we ventured out alone, we must remain within eyesight. However, as a group we could explore the grounds by following the bike path to the back of the campus. The wind propelled us forward as we pedaled vigorously, shedding the pressure from our intense studies.

Back in our rooms, we changed into our sweats, then there was a knock at our door.

Kit answered, and there stood Christan, making a funny face asking, "Friend or foe?"

Kit and I burst into laughter, and Aiden and Amaya joined in. We chatted about our day, making faces and laughing until our stomachs hurt.

Time passed quickly, and I reached for my phone to call Mum and Mimi. Both were happy that I was adjusting quickly and felt comfortable there. It was great to have a peer group.

I dressed for bed and chose not to discuss my test scores. I likely had the lowest, but as I clutched my locket, I thought about Rie and found comfort knowing that she had had similar experiences during a turbulent time.

As was pointed out to me earlier when I responded to the Key Challenges, my character was a critical component. Now was not the time to become competitive, but to be courageous, trustworthy, perceptive, and compassionate. Character counts, not competition. Feeling more confident, I fell asleep.

Before Amaya and Kit woke, I quietly left my bed and took a shower. Curious, I wondered what surprise the instructors had planned. While I brushed my teeth, Amaya and Kit called out and soon were dressed as well. We met Christan and Aiden in the dining room and consumed a healthy breakfast of eggs, muffins, and fruit.

Once in the classroom, Mr. Dunbar instructed us to open our laptops. At the top, we saw "*Quiz*." Gulping, I took a deep breath, touched "Open," I and found that we had fifteen minutes to complete twenty-five situations and facial expressions related to deceptive behavior. Carefully reading each question, I responded quickly to each situation.

"Time!" Fifteen minutes sped by, for sure. The computer would provide an immediate score, so I touched the response and saw that I had earned a perfect score of *100%!* Mr. Finney checked and acknowledged, "Well done, trainees! Let's review your answers."

Following the quiz, we spent more time going over body language and facial responses. Our discussion was thorough, and as previously learned, each of us knew that none of the questions would be a trick, and certainly, correct answers were what we had chosen.

"You all have outdone yourselves!" Mr. Dunbar exclaimed. "Now for the surprise that we have planned. Tomorrow, you will head to London. Remember, you either must stay in pairs or a threesome. Mr. Finney and Ms. Beatty will accompany you, and Mr. Berry will drive you. After breakfast, we will leave. Dress comfortably but avoid wearing any identifying clothing."

Since the weather was clear and cool, we had an early dinner followed by some card games outside on the patio. Christan, who lived in London, gave us a map and shared some points of interest. He, Aiden, and Amaya decided that they would stay together and explore some historical sights, while Kit and I planned to check out the market and shops.

As we dressed for bed, Kit hugged Scot (her oversized cat) while I cuddled with Babbitt. Amaya popped in again, wearing her fluffy animal hoodie. Each of us hung our hoodies, jeans, and shirts on our doors to prepare for tomorrow.

"Do you think Mr. Berry is the head of BETA?" asked Amaya.

Shrugging, I said, "Maybe, he does seem quite mysterious." Kit just giggled.

I called Mum and Mimi, informing them that our group would be heading to London tomorrow, and I'd be shopping with Kit.

Mum advised, "You've been there before, but the market gets crowded, so stay together and have fun!" After sending my love, I bid them goodnight.

After breakfast, we piled into the limo with Mr. Dunbar, Ms. Beatty, and Mr. Berry driving. We shared our itinerary, and Ms. Beatty informed us that we needed to check back at the meetup area by three. Our phones were charged, and we had money in our backpacks, along with some water and snacks.

"Lunch is on your own. Have fun and stay together." Each of us updated our map connection with the meetup site and headed off.

Christan, Aiden, and Amaya planned to explore a historic building and tower. Kit and I walked to the Market, following the noise and aromas. Fortunately, Kit was wearing a headdress of colorful scarves, so I figured that I would not lose sight of her.

As soon as we took off, I knew Kit was a pacer while I was a browser. We started off together, but soon she moved ahead.

"Kit, slow down; I want to check out the street vendors."

"Look all you want; I will be just ahead in some shops." She was soon off, and I saw her enter a shop down the path.

Nibbling on some pastry and taking my time, I found a lovely cart with beautiful jewelry. I tried on some and picked out two bangles for Mum and Mimi. As I turned around, my direction seemed off. I walked toward where I thought Kit might be, but she was not in the shop.

Looking down at my phone, my map seemed wonky. The air seemed cooler, and I felt a breeze. *"Was I approaching the river?"* Remembering our class discussion about how our brain can cause anxiety, I tried to remain calm by pausing to take in long deep breaths. When the mist started to form, I felt confused. *Try not to panic,* I thought.

I recalled when I was little and got lost on the beach, and thick fog rolled, and Grandpapa told me to stop and think and get my bearings. I looked ahead and believed I saw bright scarves. *Kit?* I thought. All of a sudden, I heard my name. *"Allie, over here!"* I followed her voice and then in another direction, heard her voice and then heard, *"Allie!"* Turning again, I followed the colorful scarves. "Kit?" My heart was racing as the mist formed coils of fog curling up my legs. I struggled to move and thought that I might faint.

Clutching my locket, I knew that I had to turn around. Breaking through the fog, I saw Kit. "Allie, where were you? I saw the fog and worried."

We hugged and headed back to the meetup area. I knew I would need to share what happened since I wasn't sure exactly what had taken place in the Market.

Christan, Amaya, and Aiden had chosen to visit a historic house set in a more remote area. No one other than the three was checking out the massive home, and Christan remarked that some locals believe that it is haunted. Exiting swiftly, they decided to explore the nearby tower. The tower, which was used in the past during the war to look out for approaching enemy planes, was a few yards from the house and looked creepier to Amaya.

At the entryway, she looked up at the winding stairs and decided to wait for them, so she sat down, leaning against the wall. Both boys turned on their phone flashlights as they entered and climbed upward. There were some openings that provided natural light, but as Christan continued up, his flashlight failed. Calling to Aiden for some light, he heard no response. All of sudden, Christan thought he heard Aiden from above calling him upward. Christan, confused, thought, "That's not possible. Maybe he is calling, and I was hearing an echo."

We heard pebbles fall. Uncertain of the structure, Christan froze. He knew he was up higher than he wanted to be, and then he thought, *Where was Aiden?*

Aiden's flashlight had also stopped working, but he was not as high up as Christan, so he felt his way down toward the opening.

Seeing Aiden, Amaya asked, "Where's Christan?"

Dismayed and grimacing, Aiden commented, "He is somewhere stuck up the stairs!"

Amaya looked like she might start to cry. Aiden held his hands up, shaking away her sobs.

"No tears, please! Look for a stick, and I will try to use my fire skills. If you start crying, you will cause them to fizzle."

Finding a stick, Amaya gave him a scarf to tie around the top. Thinking hard, he saw fire in his mind and, with the stick held out, flames erupted.

"Amaya, you stay here, and I will help Christan."

The fire lit the way, and now Aiden could see the stairs. "Christan, do you see the light?"

Christan looked down and saw some light, smelling fire.

Aiden approached cautiously and finally saw Christan, who looked relieved.

"Be careful and hold on to the wall as you follow me down."

Once down, Christan was astounded that obviously, Aiden had somehow started the fire. Outside, he watched Amaya stand and appear to concentrate on the torch, then saw water flowing and extinguishing the fire. Christan was amazed to witness the twins' abilities.

Now it appeared that both phones were working again, and all three walked to their rendezvous. They saw Allie and Kit waiting with Ms. Beatty and Mr. Dunbar. Christan was sure that he had heard Aiden calling him upward, "But what had happened in the tower?" he thought.

He knew Kit and Allie would be enthralled by his account of Aiden and Amaya's skills of fire and water. "I wonder how their adventure panned out. I hope they did not experience any ominous moments like him. I guess he might need to share his experience to get some feedback," he thought.

Allie looked somewhat pale when Aiden arrived with Amaya and Kit. "I wonder if Allie was reading my mind," he thought. *He knew the ride back to the Academy would be a lively journey.*

Mr. Berry arrived, and we all piled into the limo. "How was your time at the Market, Allie? Kit?" Ms. Beatty asked.

Kit chimed in, rushing through her remarks. "Allie got lost, the fog rolled in, and our directional map was off, but we found each other!" Flushed with excitement, Kit raced through my experience.

"That's true, but perhaps the fog threw me off since I thought that I heard Kit calling me, and I couldn't see her, nor find her."

I didn't want to elaborate, knowing that my anxiety during my time lost was not a story I wanted to discuss at this time. Perhaps later when we five were together. I survived, and nothing serious happened.

"What about you three?"

Christan shared that, "While in the tower, our flashlights failed without any cell connection, and I thought that I heard Aiden calling me from above, but that wasn't possible. I guess that darkness and fog can be deceptive. My fear of heights almost paralyzed me, but Aiden and Amaya came through!"

Christan chose not to disclose Aiden and Amaya's incredible use of their skills but planned to discuss this with his five pals. "Surely, Allie experienced something most likely connected to her fears. Lots to talk about for sure," he thought. Mr. Barry and Mr. Dunbar seemed to be taking all our information in stride; however, I thought that I could pick up on Ms. Beatty's thoughts. She was concerned.

Back at the Academy, and overwhelmed with excitement, we realized that with all that happened, none of us had eaten lunch today. Fortunately, there was still a deli spread in the dining room. Trays placed over ice were abundant with meats, cheeses, salads, fruit, and my favorite, deviled eggs. Chips, breads, and sweets were there for the choosing. After one more bite of a peanut butter cookie, I was satisfied. Full, I decided to stop in the Library before heading upstairs.

THE LIBRARY: THE MANUAL

Jane Leazer

OUR HERITAGE REVEALED

THE LIBRARY KEY HUNG ON AN OLD CHAIN. There was a noticeable click as I unlocked the massive door. Since I was a little girl, I always felt at home in a library. I loved to smell and touch the books. Now, I took out my second key to open the dome over the Academy Manual.

Being somewhat of a sleuth, I loved the intrigue and respected the secrecy. Reaching out, my hand felt warm as I brushed the cover. Opening the thick book, I immediately turned to Rie's photo. There was a tremendous rush of warmth, and I recalled some of the facts revealed prior to my attendance at the Academy. More might be unearthed about Rie's legacy.

Breathless, Rie's beautiful, youthful smile greeted me. I felt somewhat giddy looking down at her photo. During most of my childhood, her smile would be the first to wake me and to say goodnight. Under her picture, there was a brief summary of her amazing legacy.

Only twelve, she had been sent to the Academy from France during World War II. "Marie Dubois, BETA attendee, fled from

France. Noted as a patriot, who with her brave family saved countless French Resistance lives. While at the academy, Ms. Dubois's heroism and valor protected the Academies' continued programs serving youth from foreign nations."

When I tried to turn the page, it seemed stuck. Perhaps that is all I could glean at the moment. My heart beat faster as I pondered what exactly and how Rie served her country while at the academy. Rie had shared some of her family history; however, there was much more to unearth.

Deep in thought, I was startled by a *click*. Looking up, I saw Christan, and as he entered, he winked at me.

"Sorry to startle you. You looked miles away." I nodded and smiled.

"Today, based on my understanding of your venture with Kit, we both faced our fears and managed to survive." He made a silly grimace. I nodded in agreement, and he continued.

"I was stuck and slightly paralyzed with fear as to how high that I had climbed, and somehow our flashlights had failed. You know about Aiden and Amaya's fire and water abilities. Luckily for me, I was fortunate to benefit firsthand from them. Amazing for sure!"

"Wow! I wish I could have witnessed their abilities in person. When I became lost and was overcome by the fog, I was fearful, yet I did not use my telepathic skills to locate Kit. My greatest source was my memory of my Grandpapa's tips on what to do when overcoming a situation like today. I relied on my senses, sound, and sight. Most important was what we recently learned in class about anxiety and staying calm. It wasn't easy, but I used breathing techniques we focused on and skills I acquired from Rie. Your family has provided you with similar skills, and I am sure other than Aiden and Amaya's rescue, you employed them."

"You are right, Allie. Much of our training depends on common sense!" "Are you finished with the Academy Manual? Your Great-grandmother has quite a famous legacy and sure is pretty. I would like to check on the Chan family." I gestured to Christan to take a look. Checking the index, Christan readily found his source. A smile crept up his face when he glanced at his great-grandfather's picture. Dressed in ceremonial robes, Christan Chan, for whom he was named, stood proudly in his family-crested robes.

Out loud, Christan read, "Christan Chan's family were known to be great healers. Residing in Canada during World War II, Christan attended the Academy during World War II. He, with fellow BETA Trainees, uncovered threats and challenges to the academy and utilized his Knowledge, Imagination, character, and Loyalty to advance further training opportunities."

"Incredible! "I exclaimed. "Looks like our Grands contributed greatly to the academy's heritage. I can't wait to hear more about the Song and McLean legacies. Time for rest after this long exhausting day."

Arriving in my bedroom, I could hear both Kit and Amaya sleeping deeply. I sat out in the hall and called Mum and Mimi. Their voices suggested some anxiety. *Had the instructors shared my experience that occurred earlier that day?* I thought. I doubted that, although they had some abilities to be telepathic, I doubted that my thoughts could transmit home.

I proceeded to explain my experience without much drama, sharing how I employed strategies Grandpapa and Rie had taught me and that I also used skills I recently learned here at the Academy. Overall, I was safe, and the Instructors were nearby. On a positive note, I ended the call by telling them that I had found two surprises that I would bring home to them when our holiday began.

Sounding somewhat relieved, Mum said, "Love you so much, and hopefully no bad dreams tonight." Mimi echoed her great love for me. Exhausted, once my head hit the pillow, I was fast asleep.

I woke the next day as soft light danced across the wall. Looking around, I gathered that I had slept soundly and noticed my covers still tucked around me. Today would be a quiet, relaxing day for all of us. Thinking about yesterday, I realized that each one of us faced our fears and applied key attributes of our character and loyalty. Fortunately, Christan and I had already talked about the fears we confronted, but then I realized that Kit had not spoken about her response and its impact.

It was obvious when I found her in the Market; she was worried that I might have been lost. She had mentioned being concerned about when her parents would transport her and the possibility of them being lost forever.

I saw the fear in her eyes, and she looked pale as can be. I am sure that we will discuss her fears from yesterday's situation; after all, we were becoming the best of friends. My guess was that Aiden and Amaya were also troubled since their connectivity was interrupted. I'd wait to see when and what they choose to share later today.

Looked like everyone was sleeping late. I took a quick shower, got dressed, and went downstairs to eat some breakfast. Ms. Beatty was there and joined me.

Smiling, she said, "You and Kit handled your fears with confidence yesterday. What are your plans for today?"

Nibbling on my croissant, I smiled and said, "I wish that I could continue to check the Academy Manual. Last night some pages seemed to stick, and I was concerned that I might tear a page."

"When you finish eating, let's go in, and I should be able to help you, "she said.

Click, the key turned unlocking the Library door. Then another *click* and the dome rose off the Manual. Ms. Beatty noticed when I touched the book that I smiled.

As I clutched my locket, she asked, "Did your Great Grandmother give you your locket?" I nodded yes.

Continuing, she commented, "I can tell how special your heart locket is to you."

I was glad that Ms. Beatty didn't inquire about the inscription. Then she took out some lotion and applied it to her fingertips. The pages turned.

As I turned to the page with Rie's picture, the paragraph began with an annotation that the information was to be released in 2022.

I gasped, reading on about the facts conveyed that when Marie Dubois entered the Academy, she was known to possess telepathic abilities. I had experienced some of these abilities, but I didn't realize the extent of her skills and when they existed.

"Extraordinaire!" I knew Rie herself would exclaim, I thought. Her family had sent Marie to a boarding school, but foreign agents tried to kidnap her. Since the academy provided a protective environment and offered programs for exceptional students, she was sent to the Academy to become a BETA. Safety was of the greatest priority for her and her fellow trainees.

The pages seemed to stick again, so Ms. Beatty waved me to close the Manual and lock the dome.

"You have quite a legacy, Allie. You and your fellow trainees are here for a special reason, and each one of you will learn more about your family members, their journey, and your purpose as an individual and as a group."

I thanked her and went outside to sit in the garden. I imagined Rie those many years before facing such perilous attempts against her. *Perhaps more facts will be disclosed here, or perhaps I had to wait until I returned home to read her journal,* I thought. I could still sense her presence as if she had given me big hug.

The air was so refreshing as I relaxed in a comfy lounge chair. Soon Kit came and sat by me, as did Christan, Amaya, and Aiden.

Looking over to Kit, I said, "I was so relieved when I saw your bright scarves in the market!" She nodded and smiled. My comment opened up our discussion about yesterday.

"Yes, you know how I worry about my family when they transport, and that was a fear I experienced, imagining that Allie was lost somewhere."

Silent, we clung to each word she said. "Recently, I checked out the Academy Manual and found a picture of Katherine McLean who was an instructor during World War II. Most likely, she taught your ancestors. When the Manual was stolen, our family, the "Seekers," were able to discover where it was hidden and return it to the Academy. Obviously, there were foreign agents who planned to undermine the mission of the school. Hopefully, we can all go into the Library together and learn more about our legacies."

I recall Ms. Beatty mentioning when we first arrived the McLean's finding the Manual. *There's more to discover for sure,* I thought. Funny that Kit hadn't told me that she had visited the Library already, but neither had I.

Aiden and Amaya spoke up next, "Yesterday we used our abilities to help out a friend. Only under duress can we apply them," said Aiden.

Amaya added, "Yes, I was worried that I couldn't connect with Aiden, and Christan was missing too. I was relieved when Aiden showed up and shared that Christan was stuck, so we needed to apply our abilities."

"I wish I had witnessed what happened," I exclaimed. Kit shook her head in agreement.

Aiden continued, "We too checked out the Academy Manual and discovered a picture of Marco Song, who attended school with your ancestors. As you know, our families are inventors and chemists too. Marco invented a tablet via heat and fluid that, once mixed with water, created a fog screen or film so that nearby individuals could remain undetected. This invention assisted soldiers during the war."

"Amazing!" Kit blurted.

These inventions and their skills seem right out of a Sci-Fi movie, I thought.

"Glad everything worked out yesterday, and I know as our journey and training continues, we will learn much more about our families," I said.

Christan hadn't said much, but our discussion last night seemed to help him deal with his frustration over facing his fears.

After such an intense discourse, we chose to enjoy the afternoon tea served on Sunday. I enjoyed the proper service using teapots that were being served in delicate cups and saucers. I'm not sure if Aiden and Christan found the dainty meal as fulfilling, but they sat back and consumed every pastry available.

Afterward, we chose to take a long walk as the air had turned cooler. Later, all of us parted and readied for bed. Two weeks remained before our holiday. As our initial training would be ending, we knew our studies would become comprehensive and intense.

After a quick call to Mum and Mimi to offer reassurance that all was fine, I showered, then quickly fell asleep, and woke the next morning to the sound of the phone alarm.

TELEKINESIS: WHO CAN READ MY MIND?

EACH OF US ATE QUICKLY AND ARRIVED TO CLASS, ANTICIPATING OUR DIRECTION FOR THE WEEK. Opening my laptop, I smiled at the outline. Telekinesis was listed first, followed by Physics, and lastly, Behavior. Next to our computers were earphones and a mask. *What will happen next? I thought.*

Mr. Dunbar grinned broadly. "As you can see, we have a busy schedule this week. We are optimistic that each of you will build on the skills you possess; some are more advanced, but all will catch on and catch up. Ms. Beatty and Mr. Finney have briefly reviewed the importance of being able to clear your minds, which I know is not an easy task for a twelve-year-old, but you will. You will learn to block out extraneous information and receive clear messages."

Really? I wondered. Ms. Beatty frowned at me, most likely reading my mind. *Whoops.*

"Let's begin with an exercise. For five minutes, you will sit with earphones and a mask on. Most likely, the time will seem endless, but you can do it. Ready? Masks and earphones on. Time starts now!"

No sound nor sight was evident. These sensations felt strange and uncomfortable. This seemed to go on forever.

Finally, I felt a tap on my shoulder. We removed our masks and earphones. Mr. Finney asked me about our short-lived deprivation. Amaya spoke up, "I was freaked out, Mr. Finney, since I couldn't channel Aiden!"

Ms. Beatty emphasized, "This activity can be stressful, but we will practice this for the next few days to help you start to block out useless information. Yoga and Tai Chi will be offered after class to develop your breathing and careful movement through space. These are all important aspects to assist you with telepathic skills and later on, transporting."

Transporting! Wow! I thought. Ms. Beatty smiled again, looking right at me.

Read over the information below and continue to practice.

- Telekinesis: The ability to move objects at a distance by mental power
- Telepathy: Communication of thoughts
- Tai Chi: Slow body movements and breathing relieving stress on the body and mind
- Physics: The branch of science concerned with the nature and properties of matter and energy

After a few more deprivation trials, we took a break. Snacks of fruit, nuts, and cheese were available. Nourished, we returned to class. Now we would visually focus on a point in the room, breathe, and with our earphones on, try to pick up a message.

At first, I heard a few words. Ms. Beatty pointed to our earphones, and then on the screen were three sentences to choose from:

- Pickle relish was on the hotdog.
- Pickles were sliced on the hotdog.
- No pickle relish was on the hotdog.

I guessed the middle answer, but I only heard the first few words. I was incorrect.

"Try again," Ms. Beatty encouraged. "Breathe, focus, and put on your earphones."

In the next example, I listened intently.

- Bacon and eggs are my favorite breakfast.
- Eggs and bacon are my favorite foods.
- Only bacon and eggs are my favorite breakfast.

I chose the first answer, thinking I heard all seven words. *Yes, I was correct! Whew!* I thought.

We continued throughout the morning, and I earned 90%. Everyone scored similarly.

Mr. Dunbar praised us. That afternoon, we would listen while wearing a mask. Our brains tired, and we were directed to go and eat some lunch.

Kit exclaimed, "I'm fried. Are you?"

Everyone looked worn to the bone and shook our heads in agreement. Hungry, we gorged on stuffed potatoes, chicken, corn, and a fruit sundae.

Returning to our classroom, Mr. Finney was there to preside over our next challenge. "Masks on and breathe. Listen carefully."

Some silly thoughts invaded my concentration and muddled my answer.

"Any responses?"

Kit spoke up. "The boat is sinking in the river."

What? I thought. I heard something about the river, but no boat.

"Close," chuckled Mr. Finney. "The boat is sailing in the river."

"*I should be better in this area, but obviously not. Oh Rie, where were my Dubois telepathic abilities? Maybe I wasn't concentrating, or perhaps there was some other kind of interference. No,*" I argued with myself, and then suddenly I heard Ms. Beatty encouraging me to pay attention.

"Mask on and listen carefully. Any response?"

Almost shouting, I said, "The Queen of England invited us to tea!"

"Correct!"

As the afternoon waned, all of us continued to listen and respond with amazing accuracy.

"Great job, trainees!" praised Mr. Finney. "Enjoy dinner and be prepared to further address your telepathic abilities with your eyes and ears intact. See you bright and early in the morning!"

Feeling more confident, I clutched my locket thinking about Rie's experiences so many years before. After all, she exhibited noteworthy telepathic abilities. Hoping not to let her down, I decided I would be more optimistic about demonstrating even more accurate responses tomorrow.

I called Mum and Mimi, and I shared that we were moving forward on skills that Rie had experienced.

"Sounds like you are enjoying yourself now that each area is more focused on many of your initial challenges!" Mum said.

Mimi offered words of encouragement and ended by saying, "Excited that you will be home in less than two weeks." I would take a direct flight to Atlanta, and then they would meet me and drive me home to Charleston.

After my call, I decided to check and see if Ms. Beatty was around to look for more information about Rie. Fortunately, she was in the dining area drinking some tea. Smiling at me, she gestured for me to sit down.

"Ms. Beatty, could you help me review more information in the Academy Manual? The pages seem so delicate, so I would appreciate some assistance."

"Sure thing, I know you are even more curious about Rie's training after learning some relevant facts. It is important to seek and find the truth."

Sounds familiar, I thought.

"Let's take a look."

The lobby was quiet as we walked towards the Library. *Click* and we were in, and another *click* opened the dome. Ms. Beatty then dabbed some cream on her fingers, and the book opened again to Rie's picture.

A surge of warmth spread through me. No, I didn't imagine the tingling sensation. I am sure that I was overcome with emotions.

As the page turned, I read, "*Right before France was liberated, there was an attempt to kidnap Marie Dubois; however, the effort was thwarted by the heroic actions of fellow BETAS.*" I gasped, wondering if my new pals' family members who attended the Academy with Rie, rescued her.

Ms. Beatty remarked, "I am sure that there is more to uncover either within the Manual or possibly the journals written by your Great Grandmother. The good thing is knowing that she confronted danger and was rescued."

Nodding, I wondered how Ms. Beatty seemed to be aware of aspects pertaining to Rie. *Maybe her family also attended or instructed BETAs during Rie's presence.* She winked. Probably reading my thoughts.

"Night," I said.

Thoughts were jumbling in my brain as I entered my room. Kit was sound asleep. Soon I too drifted off. There was a vast field, and then I heard footsteps. Running ahead, I saw a figure. *"Rie, is that you?"* She kept running, and then I too sprinted, following her, while a sinister voice kept calling out, *"You'll never finish!"* The voice was deep and harsh, and his footsteps got closer. Trapped, I needed to escape, and so I ran faster, wondering *"What did I need to finish?"*

Soft light woke me from my sleep. My sheets were tumbled on the floor. *"Was my dream a premonition?"* Silly thought, so I shook it off as I showered and then hurriedly dressed.

Perhaps I was stressed like the others? as we were fast approaching our final few days before we headed home for our holiday break.

Greeting my pals, we all ate and walked together to our classroom. On our laptops, we noticed that today's focus would be more on our telepathic practice as well as physics.

Mr. Finney reported that before the week ended, we would initiate some transporting activities. All of us glanced at one another, marveling at the quickened pace of our studies.

Mr. Dunbar announced that on Friday we'd meet a substitute, Mr. Crocket. "I will be attending a short seminar, and Mr. Crocket will fill in. Not to worry, I will be back before you leave for the holiday."

For some reason, his announcement caused some uneasiness. *"Perhaps my dream had something to do with my reaction."*

As planned, we started our telepathic training using both our eyes and ears unblocked.

"Breathe, clear your mind, and focus!" Mr. Dunbar encouraged.

Nervous, I missed the first message. I heard Ms. Beatty's voice in my head sending me a strong message. *"Time to look in your heart and mind, and truth you will find, Allie."* I nodded, listened, and wrote the correct message on my sheet.

We continued our practice until early afternoon, and then Mr. Finny called us to break. He complimented us with great enthusiasm for meeting expectations.

After a short break and some nourishment, we moved to the Lab. Sitting at individual tables, we saw objects of various sizes.

Once again, Mr. Finney directed, "Clear your mind, breathe, and focus!"

We had spent some time previously utilizing principles of physics to move objects. Concentrating, I amazed myself by seeing the smaller object move. Then, to my astonishment, I moved the midsize object and successfully moved the larger one as well as our session ended. *Perhaps this was my lucky day or this was a new ability unknown to me,* I thought.

Exhausted, we took a much-needed break for lunch. Aiden and Amaya were sitting together, and I asked them, "Since you both are so connected with your thoughts, how are you able to block out your own interference?"

Aiden laughed and said, "We have been doing that for years. Even though we do pick up on each other's thoughts, we must block them at times. It takes much effort and a lot of deliberate concentration. Not so easy for sure!" Amaya nodded and smiled while Christan poked Aiden. Kit shook her head and giggled.

Feeling utterly worn out and on edge, we jumped when we saw flashing lights. *Could there be a fire?* I thought. Mr. Finney came over and told us to go to our classroom. His tone was urgent, and he appeared deeply concerned. Once inside the classroom, Ms. Beatty was already there, speaking in a hushed low tone so we couldn't overhear her conversation. As we entered, the door locked behind us.

Turning to face us, she explained, "The Academy may have been breached. We are currently conducting a search to determine if the Manual is missing. Many years ago, there was an attempt to steal the Manual, but was stopped."

As I walked toward the classroom, I noticed that the Library door was slightly ajar, an unusual occurrence as we typically had to use our key to enter.

Kit mentioned, "Earlier, I heard some noises and giggles. It reminded me of when my family thought elves had entered our home predawn. Could this be a prank or the work of mischievous elves?" Kit asked earnestly.

Despite knowing that Kit's family believed in such paranormal occurrences, her suggestion seemed far-fetched, and we chose not to comment. "Actually Kit, we are aware that paranormal events can happen. However, we highly doubt that elves are involved," clarified Ms. Beatty. She continued, "Mr. Berry is checking security, and hopefully he'll find the culprit."

Her phone rang, but since we could now pick up some of the information telepathically, each of us chose to block the message due to the sensitive nature of the conversation.

Mr. Berry soon reported back, saying, "All clear. The Manual has been located and is safely returned to the Library, securely locked under the dome. From now on, if you wish to access the Library, an instructor must be present. There has been no explanation provided for the mysterious disappearance. Perhaps we'll speculate about the possibilities later."

I was certain that our instructors were trying to minimize any concerns, and we understood that security was always a top priority.

Mr. Dunbar entered and directed, "Classes are concluded for today. Get some rest."

Climbing the stairs to our rooms, we all agreed to change into comfy clothes and ride bikes until dinner time. Donning our helmets, we chose our bikes and peddled furiously to let off steam from a challenging day. Numerous unanswered questions had been raised, but answers were still elusive, at least for now.

Security matters were not our concern, so we refrained from discussing them much until we finished our bike ride and sat outside under the stars. A buffet had been set up for us to take trays outside, and I nibbled on cheese and crusty bread.

Christan sat beside me and asked the group, "What do you think really happened this morning?"

Recalling our visit to London, my experience at the market, my dreams, and the missing Manual, I spoke up, "Perhaps there's a threat to interfere with our training."

Looking concerned, Kit added, "Maybe we need to watch out for each other." Everyone nodded in agreement, acknowledging the potential dangers.

During my nightly call to Mum and Mimi, I chose not to mention the day's events, hoping for some resolution and no further threats. Fortunately, I slept okay and woke up early as the week came to an end.

Back in our classroom, Mr. Dunbar, Mr. Finney, and Ms. Beatty were all present. Standing with them was a tall man whose reddish hair curled over his collar. He wore glasses with thick lenses, and his eyebrows seemed bushy. His attire was rather formal, consisting of a jacket, shirt, and tie.

Mr. Dunbar got our attention, introducing the man by saying, "Everyone, please welcome Mr. Crocket. As I informed you earlier, he'll be here while I attend a seminar in London. His expertise is in transport, and you'll glean much knowledge from him over the next few days."

When Mr. Crocket smiled, although it resembled more of a leer, his gaze fixed on me, and my stomach churned. I tried to block my discomfort and negative thoughts about him, but my hair stood on end.

During our break, I asked the others about their initial impressions. No one thought much about him, except that he seemed a little stuffy.

We continued our practice, moving objects of all sizes. Unhappy to see that Mr. Crocket sat in, and yes, I still felt uncomfortable. Though I tried to clear my mind, scary thoughts crept in, and I struggled with moving even the smallest objects. Ms. Beatty asked me to step out into the hall.

Checking in with me, she asked quietly, "What's up? You look tired and distressed."

Trying not to think about my reaction to Mr. Crocket, I shook my head and said, "I slept okay, but thoughts about the past, Rie experiencing similar circumstances, might be interfering with my concentration this morning."

Ms. Beatty was very perceptive, so I tried to shield my emotions and thoughts from her. *Hopefully, I was overreacting,* I thought. Together we practiced deep breathing, similar to what I would do with Rie when stressed.

Then I returned to class and was able to apply myself. During lunch, Kit asked what happened this morning. I briefly shared the account of Rie's thwarted kidnapping, my crazy dream, and my distrust of Mr. Crocket.

"Wow! Perhaps you overthink and stress yourself out. You do have high expectations of yourself, and we all know your Rie had quite a reputation here. I admit that you are a much more serious trainee than the rest of us, though we all have connections with the Academy.

We have not heard much from the others about their legacies, but you know my family was considered heroes once they located the missing Manual. Remember, we are all here for one another, especially me."

She gave me a much -needed hug and stated, "Mr. Crocket does look a bit odd, but I have no opinion yet. Like I said earlier, all of us need to keep a watchful eye." Kit's support lifted my spirits, and I, along with my fellow trainees, completed our assigned tasks.

111

Later that afternoon, after changing into sweats and running shoes, I decided to head out to the trail near the Academy for a run. The rule was that if alone outside, one must remain within eye view of the staff.

As I rounded the furthest point from the Academy, I heard a deep voice, "Allie, wait up!" *It's Mr. Crocket! No way*, I thought, as I heard his heels pounding the trail. *Why was he out here? Did he follow me? I hoped someone was watching.*

My anxiety was mounting when he yelled, "Hey, slow down, I would love to chat with you about Rie and your family!" *Did I hear him correctly?* I thought.

Turning and slowing down some, I shouted, "Not now, maybe later!" I then took off at a clip. Somewhat of a sprinter, fortunately, he was unable to catch me. Out of breath and panting, I ran into Kit and Amaya.

Amaya looked startled. "What's up, Allie?"

"Had a little run-in with Mr. Crocket!"

She looked puzzled. "Not sure what he knows about each of us and our family connection with the Academy, but he brought up Rie."

I could tell that Kit was processing my comments and said, "That seems strange, Allie."

Speaking to Mum and Mimi that night, they asked if everything was fine. *Perhaps Ms. Beatty had called them*, I thought. So I said that I was a little stressed out due to the intensity of our training, but otherwise all right. I fibbed just a bit. I was happy that I would see them in about a week. Once my call was finished, I saw Christan motioning me to come out.

"Let's chat with Kit, Aiden, and Amaya. Kit mentioned that you felt uneasy with Mr. Crocket. What's up?"

Pulling some cushions together, I shared my experience and my dream. My dreams at times seemed to be a premonition, at least that was my past experiences.

"I recall those red flags we discussed during our behavior training, and actually, he fits the bill of a scary guy!"

Aiden started to chuckle, but abruptly stopped when Amaya glared at him.

"Remember, Aiden, Mr. Finney, and the other instructors said we should always respond to our gut reactions. Let's make sure that, as Kit said, we all keep an eye on him and watch out for one another!"

"Sure thing, Allie! We understand how you feel and will support you!" So in agreement, we placed our hands over one another in a circle like a pledge. I slept better that night knowing my pals had my back.

Kit had opened the windows, and I woke up to birds chirping. The sounds of the birds were always welcoming and provided a sense of optimism. The sky was almost cloudless, and a cool breeze tousled the sheer drapes.

"Please arise and shower, Princess Allie," Kit mocked with a curtsy.

"Your breakfast awaits!" She laughed loudly.

Crossing my hands over my heart, I gestured, saying, "You are in a good mood." I tossed Babbitt at Scot, who Kit was snuggling.

"Should be a cool day, so wear a hoodie over your t-shirt."

"Thanks, Mom" I curtsied back.

Down the stairs, we went and met up with Aiden, Amaya, and Christan. Today would be a well-deserved fun day with outdoor games and a picnic. I chose a hot breakfast of eggs, cheese grits, a chocolate croissant, and a good cup of hot tea, as Mum would say. We marched outside. Standing together were Mr. Berry, Mr. Finney, Ms. Beatty, and the dreaded Mr. Crocket. *If teams were assigned, I would definitely not be on team Crocket!* I thought.

Actually, the teams comprised of Trainees, Mentors, and Instructors. The Mentors were split between the two groups. Sounded fair to me, and I was relieved too. We played kickball, volleyball, and lastly tug of war.

I found myself at the front of the line, tugging against Mr. Crocket. His glare looked almost menacing, and I tried to avoid looking into his eyes.

"Pull!" said Robert, one of the mentors who stood at the end of our line.

Suddenly, a flock of hostile birds flew over, cawing loudly. *Did someone conjure up the hostile birds?* I thought. Maybe that caught Mr. Crocket off guard, as when we pulled, he fell over the line and pulled his team down.

Our team cheered!

He grimaced and smirked, so I hurried onward to the picnic area. The tables were filled with tasty treats and gourmet food. The chef outdid himself with such a bountiful spread.

Full, we played some card games, and I did my best to avoid eye contact with Mr. Crocket.   About two hours had passed, and I felt a need to go for a run.

"Anyone want to join me on the trail?" Waved off by my friends, I stretched and started to jog at first.

As I rounded the first leg, I heard shoes heavily pelting the ground behind me. A guttural, almost growl shouted my name.

"Allie!"

I knew Mr. Crocket was chasing me. Negative thoughts were being shot at me like a piercing arrow. *You are nothing like Rie! You are a failure! My dream is coming true! How could this be happening? I thought.* I had already experienced questionable behavior by him. Trying to escape him, I crossed the grounds, no longer within eye view of the group. He was closing in, taunting me.

"Who are you?" I yelled at him.

He was cackling an almost growl. As he closed in, I felt his hot breath and heard his clanking cleats as we both rounded the farthest portion of the trail.

No! I thought as I panicked. A mist was creeping in from the stream, and a coil of fog was twisting around me.

"Stay away!" My voice sounded hoarse, and my heart was beating so fast. Through the mist, I thought that I was moving in the direction of voices, and then... All was black!

"Allie!" Familiar voices, seeming distant, were calling my name.

Someone was shaking me, and then I was lifted and carried into the Academy. Smelling salts revived me, and then I felt a cold compress on my head.

A doctor had been called, and he, after arriving, checked my vitals. Thankfully, upon checking, there was no sighting of Mr. Crocket. The doctor ordered for me to remain in the infirmary and drink some Gatorade.

He diagnosed that I was dehydrated and needed to stay in the infirmary overnight. Ms. Beatty came in and patted my hand, clearly aware of my trauma. *Was she reading my mind and picking up when Mr. Crocket was taunting and threatening me?* I thought.

She whispered, "He's gone from campus, banished."

Relieved, I slept through the afternoon. Christan, Kit, Aiden, and Amaya were allowed to check in for a quick visit.

"You gave us quite a scare," said Christan.

"Thankfully, Kit saw you running with Mr. Crocket not far behind. She alerted Mr. Finney and Mr. Berry, who found you passed out. Mr. Crocket disappeared or was kicked out, we presume. You went to great lengths to banish him," he grinned.

Ms. Beatty shooed them out, and I fell back to sleep.

Ms. Beatty entered my darkened room in the infirmary and gently woke me. "I spoke to your Mum, as did the doctor. I conveyed somewhat about what you previously shared and the incident this afternoon. They know about Mr. Crocket, and I assured them that you were and are not in any present danger. Do you feel that you are safe and want to remain here until your holiday?"

I nodded in agreement. "Give them a call and reassure them that you plan to stay here and finish this session before your holiday." Smiling, she handed me the phone, and I called Mum and Mimi.

"Hi sweet girl," Mum spoke gently to me. Her calm voice soothed me. I was comforted hearing her and Mimi in the background declaring their love for me.

My voice faltered when I spoke, "I understand that Ms. Beatty told you about today's occurrence. I have been dreaming as I do sometimes, and Rie has been at the forefront. When I return home, I plan to read more of Rie's journals since I have some ideas about her perilous life during World War II. Being able to check the Manual here has helped with more of my understanding. There are lots of facts that I, and my fellow trainees, are sorting through and piecing together. Know Kit plans to visit, so I am sure she'll share more about her family's role. I won't speculate about Mr. Crocket, and I remember Rie's affirmation that I can find truth when I look within my heart and mind. The training is intense and challenging, but the instructors are supportive, as are my cohorts. All is well, and I will rest tomorrow, as we are getting ready for our final week before I come home for our holiday."

Mum sounded okay, and as she and Mimi hung up, I was so grateful for their understanding and support. I clutched my locket and could only imagine the multiple challenges that Rie faced.

116

Sunday, I rested and saw the doctor, who cleared me. He ordered quiet activity but allowed me to return to my room. Kit and Amaya had gotten me flowers, and the guys had created a funny card that made me chuckle out loud. All was right in the Reddinger world.

"Thanks, guys, for your support. I am so thankful that Kit spied on Mr. Crocket following me. I know that I have quite an imagination, but I do think he was taunting me."

They all agreed, and I hugged each of them. *Did Christan just blush?* I thought.

TELEPORTING: TIME TRAVEL?

AFTER ALL MY REST, I DIDN'T THINK THAT I WOULD SLEEP, BUT I DID. I WOKE UP READY FOR THE DAY. Opening our laptops, our weekly schedule was outlined. On Monday, we would practice moving objects telepathically, practice physics, and spend ample time with deep breathing control, as well as Tai Chi. The gentle art of Tai Chi would allow us to move our bodies gracefully through space.

Tuesday and Wednesday were days focused on transporting. *Were two days sufficient?* I thought. Guess the Academy thought so. Thursday would involve a major transporting exercise, and Friday, a day of debriefing.

As we entered the lab, I noticed rather large objects sitting on the tables. Each of us sat on a stool. Boy, was I happy to see Mr. Dunbar back again.

Giving us a thumbs up, he stated, "Glad to be back. Are you ready to focus? Now concentrate! Breathe! Move the object!"

I heard deep breathing, and then slowly the large objects moved.

Grinning, he gave us a thumbs up. "Again!" he directed.

We continued this practice with larger objects and then finally took a break. "Great job!" Now we received two thumbs up.

"After lunch, we will discuss principles of transporting."

Hungry, I checked our lunch meal and saw that we had lots of food for the brain, with various kinds of fish available. We enjoyed, especially British fish and chips.

Back in class with laptops open, we read on top:

Transporting Principles
Wormholes: Interstellar gateways allowing us to travel instantly through space
- From one point to another
- Are generally small, but large ones have been found
- Can allow a body to transport swiftly through space and time and materialize.
- Look like large black masses
- Transport can occur with a large boost factor
- Negative energy allows the two points in space to collide enabling an individual to transport.

"You have worked on physics concepts that allow you to concentrate, breathe, and move objects. Now you each will use your knowledge and skills to apply these principles to move objects through space. Don't worry; this will be an incredible and swift process. We will show you on the screen how this works."

A video opened up on our screens, demonstrating the process.

Kit looked apprehensive, realizing that the potential for getting lost was her greatest fear. I glanced at her and squeezed her hand. Her confidence always astounded me, and now I recognized that she too, like the rest of us, needed to overcome her biggest fear.

Mr. Dunbar continued, "Our practice will be held inside. Baby steps for sure! Watch the screens that demonstrate the physical attributes as they occur. We promise that no one will vaporize!"

Everyone looked startled and surprised, and then he and Ms. Beatty chuckled. Nervous, I am sure, but we had complete faith in their analysis.

We watched intently as Mr. Dunbar entered the portal. As he stood straight, a visual field was present, and then a bright light. Now he appeared to be on the opposite side.

Amazing! I thought.

Ms. Beatty walked in and stood still. Once again, you could observe a faint field and then a bright light. She too stood on the other side.

Wow! How was that possible? I thought.

They both exited the capsule and asked, "Questions?"

Endless inquiries were tossed their way. "How?" "What do you feel?" "Is it painful?"

Ms. Beatty smiled, saying, "We have achieved this ability resulting from scientific endeavors, and Kit, you know firsthand the possibilities since your family has perfected this ability for generations."

Their answers seemed to lessen our fears, but until we tried, I doubted we would possess any confidence.

Looking at my phone, the time was close to 4:00. We would sit there for countless hours trying to surmise the magical aspect of transporting, but as they said, no magic, just physics!

Ms. Beatty sent us on our way, reminding us, "Study your notes and come prepared to transport tomorrow."

Later, I chatted with Mum and Mimi. Their voices conveyed their overall relief that I sounded all right.

Challenge of The Keys

Once we all left class, we were astounded by what we had witnessed. Since Aiden and Amaya's parents were chemists and inventors, they understood more relevant aspects and appeared more open-minded. Christan, always calm, assumed the psychological viewpoint and could apply behavioral principles. I struggled to comprehend the sheer possibility of moving our bodies through space. Conceptually it made sense, but practically, I was stumped. Kit was more than panicked. Her family were seekers and could readily transport. Her recollection included hearing stories about family members being stuck someplace but eventually returning. *Could that happen to her?*

Aiden appeared more supportive and encouraging. "Ms. Beatty and Mr. Dunbar explained that you'll feel a warm and sudden movement like the wind blowing you along."

"Sounds plausible," Christan stated, shrugging his shoulders. Amaya was all in and excited, exclaiming, "I hope that I can transport with you, Aiden!" She was obviously concerned about the disconnection from him.

"Hoping for the best," I meekly responded. No comment came from Kit.

We chose to go to bed early, knowing our aptitude and fortitude would be challenged. Aside from the key attributes now gleaned from our newly acquired knowledge, now we had to delve into the traits of our imagination!

Back in our room, Kit and I said our good nights and fell asleep quickly. Now I was in a dark place. *Where was I? Kit, Amaya, are you here?* Voices echoed and bounced off walls. *Did I transport, and now am I stuck?*

I woke with my covers tossed. Surely, this dream was a result of our practice and discussion. No need to share. As I clutched my locket, I wondered, *another premonition, Rie?*

Kit looked beat. *Somehow, we needed to rally around each other and move forward, confronting our fears and challenges. Rie and all my friends' ancestors did so many years before.* Squeezing Scot, she looked younger than twelve. I threw Babbitt her way and giggled.

"We are amazing gals and can overcome most obstacles just like Katherine, your great-grand, and Rie did so many years before. Both of us can succeed and will!"

"Eventually," Kit expressed reluctantly.

After our showers and a light breakfast, we met up with Amaya, Aiden, and Christan. Their enthusiasm might have bolstered us; however, doubts started to creep in.

Dressed comfortably, Mr. Dunbar and Ms. Beatty asked, "Ready to transport?"

Mr. Dunbar began, "I am sure that you recall what you observed yesterday, and that you can see we are still in one piece."

Ms. Beatty shook her head, smiling. "You'll watch us, and then each of you will experience transporting in a controlled setting. Tomorrow we will move outside, and on Thursday, you'll experience a more extensive experience."

"Ladies first," Mr. Dunbar waved with a gracious pose. Our attention captivated, we observed Ms. Beatty standing still, observed the force field, and listened attentively to his command.

"Block thoughts! Concentrate! Breathe! Transport!"

A bright flash of light emitted, then Ms. Beatty transported, and now stood on the opposite side. Then she was transported back within seconds.

Mr. Dunbar now asked, "Anyone ready to try?"

Aiden spoke up and handed his phone to Amaya while she gave him a big smile of approval.

I thought how brave he was being the first to commit. Watching, I noticed he was breathing deeply and emptying any thoughts.

"Are you ready, Aiden?" Aiden nodded in agreement. Mr. Dunbar reached out and patted him on his shoulder, sensing his readiness.

"Block! Concentrate! Breathe! Transport!"

Listening, we heard Aiden take a deep breath and then saw a flash of light, and presto, he was on the other side. We all gave him a thumbs up. Amaya looked relieved.

Ms. Beatty inquired as to how he felt. "Share your experience with the group," she encouraged.

Jokingly, he patted his body. "All kidding aside, I felt a gentle wind and a sudden movement. Actually, I don't remember much nor seeing the bright light."

Kit and I seemed a little doubtful, but our confidence was emerging. Aiden encouraged Amaya to try, reminding her to block and vacate their twin connection. I could tell that he was conveying her to use her vast abilities that she alone could apply independently of him.

Her stride exuded confidence as she breathed deeply, almost sighing. Ms. Beatty clearly and concisely presented the directives, "Block! Concentrate! Breathe! Transport!" Within seconds, Amaya stood on the other side. She grinned broadly.

Ms. Beatty motioned for the rest of us to step forward. Reluctant, Kit and I stayed glued to our chairs, so Christan, winking at me, stepped forward. In the blink of an eye, he transported, and then all eyes turned toward us.

Ms. Beatty, detecting our hesitancy, suggested a break. Kit and I walked outside, pacing the trail, and discussed our thoughts.

"How unusual, "I declared, "that the Academy has the capability to set up this advanced system."

Kit, more of the expert, stated, "If you think about how centuries ago, scientists and astrophysicists, like Nostradamus, traveled through space, which has enabled science to advance greatly. Our Academy serves as a training school for exceptional students who are potential leaders. Any one of us could be in harm's way, and as you know, have already experienced potential threats recently. Being aware of scientific principles is critical to our understanding and safety."

Shaking my head in agreement, I commented, "Great advice! You are ever so wise, and now I suspect that you are ready for your journey."

Back to the lab area we went, feeling like subjects in a science experiment. However, we agreed that training like ours was not unusual for prospective BETAS. I watched Kit transport, and then, I bravely, took a deep breath, felt a warm push, and I too transported.

Later, during my nightly call to Mum and Mimi, our group chatted about how amazing our training had been these past few weeks. Still novices, much more advanced training would occur.

Just a few days left, and then we would be heading home. We had already shared addresses and phone numbers filed in our phone contacts, and we were going to miss each other terribly. Kit and I lived close to each other, so we already had made plans to visit one another.

Fortunately, I slept soundly, as I expected the others had as well. Today, we would venture outside to practice transporting. Now, we would need to depend on our ability to block out extraneous noise and thoughts, which was tricky for twelve-year-olds, for sure. Chatting, Amaya admitted that she was easily distracted and had to really concentrate to avoid channeling Aideen.

"Challenging for sure," commented Christan.

"Amaya, you are at a different skill level now, so everyone is confident that you can block Aiden."

Jokingly, Christan winked and teased, "Whew! I would want to if he were my brother!"

Aiden playfully poked him. In a good mood and satisfied with our fulfilling breakfast, we walked outside and joined Mr. Finney, Ms. Beatty, and Mr. Dunbar in the field nearest the first walking trail.

"Morning one and all," greeted Mr. Finney.

"Two more days of practice, and then a day to debrief before you go home to visit your families. As you know, being outside presents more challenges. Now, you must stop the sights and sounds that distract you. Watch Mr. Dunbar."

Mr. Dunbar appeared to go into a trance, and then the next moment he was down across the field. Next, Ms. Beatty transported without a hint of obvious movement.

"Practice does allow for perfection, but we just want to build your confidence," declared Mr. Finney. The guys were more than ready. Aiden was, once again, first. Looking over at Amaya, her nerves were starting to fray. He avoided eye contact and blocked her thoughts.

"What are you hearing, Aiden?"

"Birds chirping, but I can't see them."

Mr. Dunbar responded, "Right! Do you see anything in your mind?" Aiden shook his head no.

Mr. Finney directed, "Vacate and empty your thoughts and mind, concentrate, and breathe deeply. Now transport!" We barely saw a ray of light that looked more like a ray of sunshine, and then Aiden was down the field, standing by Ms. Beatty.

"Yahoo!" He shouted, as if he had crossed a finish line in victory.

Now, witnessing Aiden's success, Amaya gave it a try and, like her brother, ended up side by side. In triumph, she raised her fingers in a V for victory, and Christan successfully followed. Though Kit was a bit anxious, her nerves calmed, and she too transported.

Walking toward the point of the catapult, I clutched Rie's locket. My thoughts were jumbled, and I could see myself being chased across the field.

A taunting voice crept in, whispering, *"You are a failure, Allie!"*

"I'm not sure if I am ready," I whispered.

Ms. Beatty jogged back, and I'm sure I was pale.

Speaking directly to me with encouraging words, she said, "Look deep in your heart and mind, Allie, and truth you will find. Like Rie, you can do it! Let all those deep thoughts escape and concentrate on the task while you breathe deeply."

My mind now seemed empty, as if in a chamber. I saw and heard nothing, only Ms. Beatty's command.

"Transport!"

I felt a fleeting sensation of a gentle wind and rose swiftly, finding myself standing across the field with my friends. Not wanting to embarrass me, they still cheered. We all grinned and were quite pleased with our accomplishments.

Mr. Finney indicated that we were done for the day and that tomorrow we'd meet around dawn to complete the final session of our initial training. Feeling victorious, we marched off the field and stopped in the dining room for refreshments.

Time for milkshakes or a banana split! Once back in our rooms, exhausted, we crashed and napped until dinner time.

Christan remarked while chowing down on pizza, "I haven't napped since I was three!" Laughing, Kit agreed. Deciding that an early night was warranted, off to bed we went.

Perhaps our nerves got the best of us or the excitement of what awaited us that morning, we were all awake before the first light of dawn. As suggested, we all donned comfy clothes and met in the dining room.

"Should we pack a snack just in case?" Christan teased.

"Do you think we are heading to the great beyond?" I teased back.

"Don't think we'll transport beyond the back of the Academy, however, just in case, eat a hearty breakfast," mocked Aiden.

Amaya shrugged them off and ate light like a bird. "As I take flight, I want to lift off and not be bogged down by pancakes!" She grinned broadly.

"You all sound a little silly.," Kit expressed a tad nervously.

The unknown had raised some former fears, but I encouraged her so hopefully today's journey would be uneventful.

Fully equipped, we tromped out to the trail as the sun was rising. There was a slight chill in the air, and our breath was visible. Mr. Dunbar, Ms. Beatty, Mr. Finney, and Mr. Berry were all present.

We still wondered if Mr. Berry might actually be the Academy Headmaster, and certainly not just a chauffeur, as he always seemed to be around during the most eventful moments. They waved at us, and I noticed that they were dressed in hoodies and sweats.

Mr. Berry grinned and began in earnest, "The Academy considers each of you as exceptional Trainees who are advancing toward completion of your initial *BETA* course work. There was no doubt upon your selection that you would demonstrate excellent skills, and we applaud you for your *Courage, Character, Knowledge, Imagination,* and *Loyalty.* Your last challenge will encompass many of the skills you have acquired and that you will now apply. Are you ready to test your transporting skills?"

The still morning silence broke with our loud, enthusiastic voiced agreement, "Yes!"

"I know you're all wondering how to detect a force field. Part of that knowledge results from specific circumstances like you might face a difficult or dangerous situation. You'll find that the brain sensors will send triggers or messages that create a field through which you can transport. When you return from your holiday, those aspects of physics will be addressed. Today, the Academy will create a field again, and you'll transport a little further distance from yesterday. We don't wish you good luck because we know you can do it!" Mr. Berry advised in a confident and assertive manner. We all now realized that Mr. Berry was much more involved in the Academy's workings.

Though the sun was rising, shadows painted the field, and there seemed to be an eerie stillness. Normally, birds would welcome the day, but there was no chirping, only silence.

No one appeared alarmed by the quiet and emerging shadows, so I just framed my mind with the notion that I would and could transport. I prepared to vacate my thoughts and concentrate as I walked to our outpoint of lift-off.

"Ready, Aiden?"

He disappeared, and Amaya followed. We knew that they had transported beyond our sight and not hearing anything, we anticipated joining them upon completing our transport. Kit proceeded in front of me and, after a thumbs-up, vanished from my view.

Confident, I took a deep breath and recalled a rush of wind, some light, and then darkness! *Where was I?* Trying to get my bearings, I felt some lumpy rock-like walls. It was pitch black and cool, and I suspected that I might be underground. Catching my breath and hearing voices, I called out, "Kit? Aiden? Amaya? Christan? Are you here?"

"Follow my voice, Allie! We're all here," Christan calmly spoke. I slowly moved forward toward the voices and collided with Kit.

"Is everyone OK?" Aiden expressed concern. Speaking up, he said, "I am a little sore. I think I hit the rocky wall when I landed. Most likely we are in a cave."

Amaya now shared, "Do you think this is just a test, and they know where we are located?" Calm as ever, Christan communicated softly, "I doubt this is a test. Maybe we went through a force field. Most likely, they can track us, but we need to resolve our dilemma. I think that I can feel a draft, so we need to move in that direction."

Remembering my dream, I tried not to think this was a trap, and that we might be stuck for some time. Thank goodness there was some air available. I needed to shut out these dark thoughts and focus on our escape. I clutched my locket, knowing the truth we would find. Christan had a plan, and we needed to follow it.

"Our cells won't connect, so our flashlights won't work either. Aiden, it seems like we need your help. Feel around for a stick and use one of Kit's scarves to be a foil for fire."

Guess now Kit and I will experience Aiden's remarkable skills, I hope.

Aiden called out. "Found one, so Kit, wrap your scarf around the top."

We wished that we could witness his creation of fire, but alas, it was too dark. Amaya was starting to sniffle, and Aiden warned her to stop since his fire abilities could be thwarted. Kit and I comforted her.

"Sorry, Aiden."

As Aiden concentrated, we started to smell a burning odor, and then a flame appeared! Then Aiden took the lead, and we all followed behind.

"The draft is stronger, and I see some light!" Christan exclaimed.

"Yes, I see the opening!" Aiden held out the torch, and we saw a sliver of an opening.

"Nuts," Kit exclaimed in disgust. "No one can fit through!"

I had another thought since transporting resulted in our dilemma.

As Aiden put down the torch, clutching my locket, I suggested, "Why don't we transmit our skills and move the opening."

"Crazy idea, Allie," Amaya replied, dismissing my suggestion. "We can't move the entryway!" She was sniffling again, and Aiden warned her to stop. We still needed the torch's light, and her tears might extinguish it.

Christan spoke with authority. "Great idea, Allie! Surely we can use our knowledge of physics and move it more!"

"I'm in," said Kit.

The torch flickered, and we feared that the light might go out, so we needed to put forth our best effort. Hearing Rie's words about *"truth I will find,"* I clutched my locket.

Now was the time to be courageous and put our minds to the task at hand.

Encouraging and directing us, Christan said, "Let's stand in a line, and on 3, concentrate on moving the opening. "1-2-3! Concentrate!" *Was there a slight movement?*

"Again! 1-2-3! Super! Do you see it? The opening is widening!"

"Great!" Kit shouted.

"I think that I can squeeze through." She wriggled, and Amaya and I followed.

Outside, we girls focused again and saw the entry widen, allowing Aiden and Christan to climb out. Aiden still held the flaming torch, and then we watched in awe as Amaya held out her hands, and then water flowed, extinguishing the flame.

When we turned towards the Academy, we saw hands waving, now assuming our instructors had spotted us. Mr. Berry and Mr. Dunbar reached us first. They both looked relieved. When Mr. Finney and Ms. Beatty arrived, they hugged us. That hug comforted me.

Amaya spoke up, "Did you know where we were?"

Nodding, Ms. Beatty expressed in her cool and calm tone, "Our locator detected your location. The academy is aware of underground tunnels, but where you landed, surprised us.

We'll check and see if there was some field interference that occurred with your transporting. Let's head back for some hot chocolate or hot tea."

Shivering now from the cold and nervousness, Ms. Beatty wrapped heavy quilts around us as we started to warm up in front of the roaring fire. All of us were quiet as the events of the day sunk in. Drinking our hot tea and hot chocolate helped us to relax.

With our instructors absent, Kit asked, "Do you think we were in danger?"

Shrugging my shoulders, I replied, "Perhaps, an unknown individual or force interfered with our transporting and steered us off course! Strange things have happened."

My dream crept in again, and it was difficult to get rid of it, so I clutched my locket tightly.

Aiden scoffed, "After Mr. Crocket left, do you think everything could be a plot!"

Glaring now, Christan chastised Aiden saying, "Remember, Allie had a terrifying experience, and we don't know Mr. Crocket's motives, so back off!"

Aiden looked stunned. "Hey guys, I don't think Mr. Crocket was involved. I do get suspicious easily, but I am grateful that you all were there with me, so we were able to escape our plight together."

"Sorry, Allie, I was startled and frightened like everyone else, so forgive my reaction. Perhaps we will learn more later or figure it out ourselves!" Aiden smiled apologetically.

Leaving, both Kit and Amaya hugged me, and Christan winked twice.

Back in our room, Kit brought up my comment.

"Do you think that Mr. Crocket was involved?"

Exasperated, I shrugged and said, "Maybe. I had that crazy dream about either me or Rie, and he seemed to know more about her. I hope his being here was just a coincidence. Hopefully not!" I muttered. *Only time will tell*, I thought.

Mum and Mimi called, and I chose not to disclose any events of the day. I'd wait until my arrival home, not knowing if they were informed by our instructors.

Waking the next morning, I was surprised that I had not had any bad dreams. My covers looked as if I had not moved since my head had hit my pillow. Ms. Beatty met us in the dining room, informing us that after breakfast, we should pack and come into the lounge area.

Off we went, and the realization of leaving hit me hard. Kit lived close enough that we could visit, but Aiden and Amaya resided in California, and Christan lived here in London. Thank goodness for Facetime and Zoom chats. Two weeks wasn't forever, but it sure seemed that way to me.

Kit and I checked our drawers and closet, making sure all was secure in our suitcases. Mr. Berry loaded up the limo that afternoon. We decided to leave a note and a book to ensure our return.

As time faded, we met in the dining room for lunch and sat with our instructors and mentors. Cushioned chairs were pulled around, while we settled in, enjoying our now-established familiarity.

BETAS

MR. DUNBAR CLEARED HIS THROAT. "Attention, BETAs!" he smiled broadly. "I am sure, looking back, you are amazed by your journey starting when you received your first letter inviting you to participate in the Challenge of The 4 Keys. Having responded to The Keys of Character, Knowledge, Imagination, and Loyalty, you each received your key of Acceptance and were able to enter the Academy. Bravely, you traveled far and embarked on an incredible journey. Within a short period of time, you each developed and acquired astounding skills based on your application of traits representing The 4 Key Challenges. You arrived, bringing with you an amazing legacy of your ancestors, and discovering a connection to the past. When you return, you'll find out more about the past and how it connects with the here, now, and the future. At times, you faced challenges, but your character and loyalty to each other pulled you through. Your progress is exemplary, and all of us are so proud of you and your progress."

Each instructor applauded us.

"Now share with us a final thought about your personal experience thus far."

Aiden coughed as he cleared his throat, "Amaya and I are so connected being twins, and in the past, this is how we are identified. We even depend on our remarkable skills as a result of our connectivity. Being twins allows us to do wonderful things, but here, we are able to demonstrate our individual strengths."

Amaya nodded and shared, "Yes, I love being a twin. However, sometimes I feel overwhelmed by him. Aiden is strong, and I respect that. At the Academy, you allowed me to be myself and show my independence."

Next, Christan, looking serious, replied, "I never experienced such camaraderie. Though I know a lot about psychology and behavior, I discovered more about myself and the importance of working together."

"I confronted my fears," shared Kit. "That is, my family being transporters, I always feared they would either be stuck or lost, and my confidence did build to comprehend that I was able to transport successfully. Being able to transport is an amazing skill to possess if used wisely. I'm glad, I could share my fears and the experience itself."

Now it was my turn to share.

"Before I learned that I would attend the Academy, I received a letter from my Rie. We shared many similarities, including telepathic abilities. She had recently passed and left a letter for me and a special gift, my locket. In her correspondence, she informed me that a journey awaited me. You have watched me clutch my locket frequently, perhaps channeling her message to look into my heart and find the truth. Fortunately, I had a chance to read a few excerpts from her journal, but not until I saw the Manual did I learn about her connection to the Academy, as each of you discovered, your ancestors are connected too. Being here has enabled me to unlock the past, confront some fears, and contemplate the future. I have looked in my heart and mind and found the truth, and so will each of you!"

Smiling, Ms. Beatty handed each of us a small box wrapped with a gold ribbon. Opening it, we all grinned with pride, taking out and placing the BETA insignia on our lapels.

"Congratulations, BETAS!"

Claps and high fives followed.

Before I left that morning, Christan handed me a card. "Happy Birthday, Allie! I will call you later tonight when you arrive home."

He hugged me and winked. I blushed a bit and was ecstatic about our budding friendship.

Kit just shook her head and giggled. At the airport, Aiden and Amaya headed to their gate after Kit and I hugged them farewell. Each gave me a card.

"We will celebrate your birthday when we return."

I laughed and said, "I will miss you both for sure!"

Now on our plane, the flight attendant alerted us to fasten our seatbelts, and the plane sped down the runway.

Yes, we BETAs were heading home for a well-deserved holiday. I knew more awaited us as I would continue to seek my truth, and we'd return to master the Challenges of The 4 Keys.

ABOUT THE AUTHOR

AUTHOR JANE F LEAZER
AUTHOR GREW UP IN A FAMILY
OF STORYTELLERS.

Over the years, Jane wrote stories and poetry for friends and family. When her grandchildren were born, each year on their birthdays, she wrote each child a story. When Gracie was turning eleven, she wrote about being a wizard in training. Upon completion, Gracie and Mimi collaborated and wrote the Challenge of The Keys about five amazing trainees. Though this talented grandmother has written countless stories, this book is her first official publication.

Made in the USA
Columbia, SC
01 July 2024

b0d544fe-bae4-49ac-b3ac-28e426df7494R01